Russ

OTHER TITLES IN THE *MASKS* SERIES

DREAMING OF DEAD PEOPLE

DREAMING OF DEAD PEOPLE

Rosalind Belben

SERPENT'S
TAIL

The publishers thank Kathy Acker, Mark Ainley, Martin Chalmers, John Kraniauskas,Bob Lumley, Enrico Palandri, Kate Pullinger, Antonio Sanchez for their advice and assistance.

British Library Cataloguing in Publication Data
Belben, Rosalind.
    Dreaming of dead people.
    I. Title.
    823'.914   [F]

ISBN 1-85242-150-9

First published 1989 by
Serpent's Tail, Unit 4, Blackstock Mews, London N4

Printed in Great Britain by
WBC Print (Bristol) Ltd.

The text of the medieval poems is taken, with amended punctuation, from *The Oxford Book of Medieval English Verse*, edited by Celia and Kenneth Sisam. The quotation on page 74 is from Gerard Manley Hopkins, letter to Robert Bridges, 1st September 1885; that on page 32 from Arthur Ransome, *The Picts and the Martyrs*.

for the kindest and most patient of friends

DULAN BARBER

AT TORCELLO

The English family walked with me from the landing-stage, to the small, green piazza. It was impossible for us to lose each other, there was not the time, or the room, we had arrived on one boat and would leave on the next. It was late afternoon in the winter, a wonder there were tourists at all.

I saw the crippled rat cross the cottage garden. An old woman and a little girl were killing a fowl hung up on the washing-line by its legs, sticking the throat. The large white wings flapped very very slowly. The woman hesitated, catching the sound of foreign voices, coming along the hard path. Soothing words were spoken to the dying bird, whose blood dripped to the bucket. The child murmured. The tourists may have blenched slightly, taken aback.

I can kill if I want to eat. Though not so lovingly.

It was a poor garden. I had never in my life seen such a miserable rat. Nothing was growing; nothing, I noticed with shock, had been planted; and the ground wasn't fallow, it was waste, it was covered in rank grasses which after a small frost toppled and leaned at angles to the sky; the fence was a fossil through which the rat crept. To the visitor, no one, it seemed, bothered to cultivate their fields and gardens. I was amazed at the lethargy, the despondency of the people. I raged. It was derelict, the island. It disturbed me.

3

The canal's water was dull of eye, shifting in the wind. The wind was cold; the air like a potato crisp hurt the gums if breathed the least gluttonously.

There was then a bridge, to fields on the other side of the canal, at right of our path; and two men talking; and two dogs. A spaniel bitch heavily in whelp.

I wish I didn't understand the expressions of animals.

This she wriggled her tail, and besought me with her shyness, from where she sagged, on the hump of the bridge. I made a noise at her and she approached to be patted.

The family was following. They perhaps didn't understand dogs. The boys quietly squawked. The mother exclaimed and held the baby higher as the dog brushed her legs.

Over the rise, the fields might have been farmed. I couldn't see. I only felt they must be pitiful.

Torcello was lush and fertile once, with crops, fruits, and vegetables. In the great flooding of 1962 Venice suffered, also the islands of the lagoon. The islands were inundated. But when the water level sank, when it receded, Venice was left paved with streets and passages, Torcello with her soil salty. It was impotent.

In my mind I walk up and down the path from the jetty to the heart of Torcello. The hen's death echoes. The water is opaque. I observe myself reflected. In that sour and barren place, a spinster, who did not wish for the dry, un-rustling grass. I weep with mortification. Yet I was extremely happy.

At the end of the path the water – the body of it – had veered, and the inlet stopped. I found myself in the piazza. Here the grass was bright and underfoot. The museum, the two churches; relics of statuary; a peep over a wall into a ruin of a formal garden, with pergole, broken columns, and roses. Closed green shutters. The family. A lounging man.

A narrower track on towards the inner stretch where the motor craft in the summer land. The island's rim. Not a fat canal, slithering under emaciated willows; but lagoon, silting the further shore nearer.

A habited, corded monk, by the brick, soft red campanile, was either planting or digging up a sapling.

The family, and I, hurried, uncertain which church, at first, was which, into Santa Fosca, the octagonal, of appearance much restored. The custodian – the lounger – arranged himself dourly to take our monies, and to switch on the electric light, at the cathedral door; of stout oak, bolts, and rivets. I wasn't sure how to expect Santa Maria Assunta.

The church building was bare. Vacant. Their children stared at the devils, at the writhing wretched on the west wall. I would have made the journey alone for the weeping madonna. It was, she was, what I had come to see.

The mosaic, in the basilica, and the plaster, is half missing. The more moving. She seemed very high, very slender. I could lick the tear from her cheek and taste the salt.

She is dressed in black and she carries God in her arms. At the centre of my world, the world which at that moment was for me Torcello.

The church, the cathedral, was battered, sanctified, breathing. Its bricks exposed, stones cold, the mosaics glowing in the semi-darkness. I long to look again.

The Teotoca Madonna isn't really so beautiful. I have a postcard of her. She has a gaze of pure beauty; it is the expression of an image which is beautifully achieved; for

5

she carries salvation, in the person of God, the Christ-child.

It could have been, in a wider sense, the promise of a spiritual life, a revelation; a God-bearing image, as Dante's Beatrice. But this madonna had tears and bore God. In her solitude, her vulnerability.

Her oval face and elongated figure dominated the atmosphere as if a thousand votive candles had been lit and flickered in invisible breezes. It was a bold stroke, putting a single Lady on that curving and enfolding wall of the apse; she stood, she hovered, with her black back to Jerusalem, on the heads of the twelve apostles.

Outside the custodian lisped in his incomprehensible Venetian dialect to a friend. The family and I, we kept a tacit distance, made smiling acknowledgement of being mutual, tourists. The tear of the Madonna — I thought she was speaking, she was dumb. She was crying.

In 1500 AD the city of Torcello housed twenty thousand souls. It was not the season, obviously; the dwellings had their eyelids down; and we had to reach the landing-stage for the five o'clock ship; the dusk and the lights; the sun soon would be setting; snuggling into the lagoon, Venice reddening; the Serenissima, most serene; the sky ribbed; the water silvery-grey, and posted, mapped in the memory, the mind. December plumes floating out of our mouths. The frost biting, hung and nipped.

And my English family had arrived. I strolled on. There was a house lit, isolated. I wandered in its direction to warm myself; and when I returned a boy was shut in the wood and glass waiting room. The water lapped at the huge tarred piles below. He had gone in and had managed to lock the door, he was not able to unlock it. I

6

broke the ice by releasing the boy, by a sliding door the parents hadn't spotted.

There was no unlocking the locked door, not by gentleness, not by force. The boat swirled in, nodded us aboard, and the waiting room remained a mystery.

The interior of the boat was empty. Italian passengers were roistering in the wheelhouse, hugger-mugger with the captain. A chill freezing on deck.

> Venice is not for me to describe. I cannot. But anyway, my attention is drawn off-centre, always to the decayed, the neglected, the perimeter of vision.

I was thinking. Unfamiliar surroundings content me. Venice was a rosy blur. *This is not the life I imagined for myself.* I have not been prepared for it. I was the daughter at home, true. But before that I was not. It should have been an interlude. And it was easily borne because I was quite convinced it would have an end. It didn't end, it went on, even after I was free, almost too free. Prison of the free. Those long years at school trained me in an attitude of mind, an independence, call it solitariness, difficult to shake off. I was brought up to be a family person, to be a home-maker; to provide and cook, though not to sew, scrub, iron or press clothes, wash or mangle. To know I should have children, and that I would ponder deeply on their welfare. Like my mother.

How . . . how can I speak from my core; there is nil. I have turned thirty-six and shall never have children. I am a shrivelled person, I have sucked myself dry; I am a figure of fun; an object for curiosity; an old maid; or I shall be, old; don't suppose I don't mind. I do mind.

7

A girl I vaguely remember, rather dense about human beings, has metamorphosed into a remorse, a female, not dense about human beings. And there she will halt. Because the adages and stock remarks, the labels, cannot be gainsaid; I have quit growing; whether or not of my own volition I haven't understood; I can't begin to understand what has happened; if I could I might accept it; I want to make sense of my life. I want to make sense of my life.

I have given, have absorbed my own vitals in feeding the self victuals; and there is a shuck of skin; a flay; that is how I feel it is; not an ounce of solid flesh; my senses atrophying. I have been wondering: have I surrendered hope.

As all bodies do I require and desire to love and to be loved; to exert myself; to be stretched; to have demands made upon me, not the kind of demands which, paradoxically, are made upon me. I should prefer not to articulate such commonplaces.

It is cumulative. I knew myself equipped to withstand it; but crashed; in the middle of the classical journey. Twelve months past I should not have had to admit to loneliness; aloneness would have been the appropriate term. Abruptly, I was lonely. A slight ache opening into a grand, raw wound, very cutting. Bother it. I was, I am, lonely.

It has happened to someone whose will, whose being is implacably against it. A mistake. A holy error. If I compare the lives of spinsters I have been acquainted with, I perceive they may be lonely: I seem to see reasons why those women were patently unsuited to lovers, and children, except by the snuff of Great War casualty lists. They were not among the fuckers of this world. Is that how

8

others see me? It's a moot point. It tantalises me.

I am tormented by my life as it is: I can be perfectly cheerful on the surface. I trust mothers haven't suspected me of crying at the sight of their babies, though indeed I have. But it has become history; there was a time when my being non-productive caused a pain, as if my womb was striving towards a cliff-edge with my mind on wonky brakes. I am still stung by the proud-cat mum who bestows her child on me to hold. I am ceased of saying I want to whelp. I might have had a child aged sixteen if it hadn't been aborted in a back street. I don't harbour regret.

Physically, then, without providing and fucking and being hugged by children, one's body deteriorates with more than age; skin, hair, warmth, cunt, the lines of the cheeks and chin and mouth and eyes. I am reduced to obtaining life from nature: a refugee.

The mind, ah, the mind. *I am not the person I could have been.* I am mentally castrated. I am not the . . . I could have done better.

But it is permitted moments of heightened awareness.

I am so intensely deprived that the touch of a human being – the desired touch – can be stunningly electric, dramatic, a gift from heaven, a bolt from the blue. If someone I care for, all of a sudden, spontaneously, catches my hand which in conversation I am waving, and holds it, I am shattered with the extraordinary pleasure of it. And if children I love fall through the barrier they can't feel into my arms, I brighten.

I am dull and lethargic, from instinct am flaming. Lucky I'm not afraid of the dark I've burnt myself out in.

I have lost sight of past and future; that is no small thing; the present is an awkward fellow. I am, subjective

9

and emotional, at the mercy of my life, my experience. Conspicuous alone; the limits of possibility drawing in like a winter evening. I find it hard to bear couples. As to childless women there are babies crawling and grinning around all the corners, to unmated, unfettered individuals there must be the apparitions of reality – constant images of togetherness. I do not stress marriage, the wedded state. A fact that most of my friends are married, but every one has his dear, or hers. I swallow evidence of companionship by the hour, the minute. I am too proud to be envious. I like it. You deserve it, people. I daresay I don't, that's neither here nor there; the effect, not the cause, is my concern.

I can remember revelling in aloneness . . . thinking – if the bomb drops, I shall be by myself, how satisfactory. I used to stand on a particular limestone ridge, on the border of Wiltshire and Dorset, and look for miles: I am, I would think, the sole figure in the landscape – how marvellous. I climbed a mountain, unfrequented by woolly-capped hikers, in the far north of Britain, the highest, the furthest, the most alone I have been, and from the cairn at the summit I drew breath in a different world, with a buzz of flies for a ghost, the blue of the lochs below, and the dab of my roof, and the bumping roads I'd driven in the early morning with eyes astray for red deer – and I thought, I couldn't be happier, thank goodness I'm alone.

I need to be alone for a substantial part of day; I am miserable feeling lonely for the whole of it.

I am not inclined to run out and chatter to shopkeepers. I cannot make anyone do. I am more complicated than I have the right to be; beggars can't be choosers.

10

In my mind I have an image of family: a man and a woman — they face away from me, they may be moving, away from me; between them their children, two or three children; with their palms clasped; the male and female bodies are bent inwards like brackets. It is distorted. They couldn't, to be realistic, walk.

In me is the distorting glass. I do see, therefore, couples. I am oblivious of anyone else. There are many couples, London streets are choked full with them. I spy caring and awareness. I disregard the unfortunate who, in their multitude, merely act out the motions of family life.

I see myself always alone.

I *am* always alone, so that isn't surprising. But I notice other people make new togetherness quite quickly; married, they separate and divorce, re-form; living out of wedlock, divide and find fresh partners, homes, loyalties. They are hybrid, or amoebic, or something. Husbands die, wives die, lo and behold, the bereaved spouses have seconds and thirds; helpings, helpmates. It is amazing. The members of their families, their siblings, are married and busy creating nieces and nephews.

I don't even see a mate I might be as fertile with. I used to; I did years ago; sub-divide; and it was terribly easy. And because I hanker to exhaust myself tending; and sharing; to have a savings bank of shared experience; to share that part of life which can be, is shareable; some of this self; what happens; what I see . . . I . . .

I am left staring gloomily at people's backs.

In the work of Edvard Munch, the jealous, the anguished, the lonely, the subjective expressionist, it is he who is the more visible, though invisible, the more felt, his is the *presence*. The faces in *The Kiss* are not blurred by

11

their loving but by the bitter green mind of an artist who would love to kiss.

In my mind, human beings together, living their lives in that indecipherable blur, represent certain abstract things: such as warmth, fire, licensed lust, tenderness, ether and elixir.

> I thought: they have pale, slightly pointed Elizabethan faces, and titian hair; the eldest boy, eager, dignified, keen, his name is Peter. And Colin, he throws his arms and legs about in a comical, vulnerable fashion, that makes my heart turn over. The small, valiant one is Kitty. They all shone, for me, brilliantly.

And though they vanished when we disembarked, the mother carrying Kitty asleep, there they were at breakfast-time. I was finished with mine, as they arrived in the dining room.

Then we began to bump into each other, in the peculiar habit of tourists in the winter months. I heard Kitty shrieking happily in the rooms of the Doges' Palace, that august ambience, invoking the wagged finger and the venomous hiss of attendants. I met them searching for suitable lunch; a sandwich, or slice of pizza; and we politely exchanged information.

I spotted them at dusk. There was a funfair on the Riva degli Schiavoni. The man, Jasper, had his back to me; either side of him, Peter and Colin, who just had come from a species of bumper car, on a fixed track, and without the bumping element. Colin held Jasper's hand. Amaryllis, and Kitty in her lap, rode the prettiest

12

merry-go-round; it had two storeys, the upper a narrow circle hemmed by a curving lattice of railings; there were bowers to sit in; below swirled the gilded horses with fine bridles, saddled camels, and elephants, ornate carriages, and swings; decorated most romantically; with quaint gallop-music; and suspended from the upper storey were wrought-iron baskets of flowers: one of these suddenly crashed, cracking only the skulls of ghost children – because the places beneath were lucky to be empty; yet I felt someone had been knocked down, it was so dangerous. Before our eyes passed Amaryllis and Kitty, round and around; oblivious Amaryllis who could not have seen and hadn't realised, the noise was drowned, smiling privately at the little girl.

I moved to the extreme edge of the water, and stared into the lagoon.

I retraced my steps, to the church at the rear; Santa Maria della Pietà. I hesitated by the square window, in the half-entrance. The altar candles were lit; incense burning; a priest saying mass; a domestic scene with Italian women in trousers and scarves. Not a tourist attraction, but touching.

I watched, and went away.

The evening was oddly balm mingled with frost. A funfair comes to the Riva always at Christmas-time, in the winter.

The family has an eccentric method of progression, in Venice, by day. I meet them head on, twice. Jasper first, alone, with map in hand, and some large guide books uncomfortably, I would have surmised, tucked under his elbow; no sign of the others; miles behind, Amaryllis and the children, at their own pace; taking in toy shop windows, all sorts of windows, stopping on bridges to examine meat boats, fruit and vegetable boats, refuse-collecting barges, to listen to some Venetian argument; so that – it is evident, inevitable – Jasper forges on with itchy legs, and waits patiently, far beyond their sight, for them to catch up; and instead of losing each other they seem to have a sixth sense; like insects performing a complex dance to imperceptible rules. It amuses me. And the children, rarely hustled, traipse long distances quite without rancour.

In the hotel, our rooms are not so far apart. It is plain that Jasper and Amaryllis are a trifle stuck. I doubt they wish it otherwise, they are devoted parents; but after supper, they bring the children in, to a late bedtime by home standards, and are confined.

The children are excited, wildly, and can't sleep. A pained American from the floor above says his wife has a migraine. It sounded jolly to me. And by our last night in Venice, I have offered, tentatively, to mind them for a while.

It was almost unnerving to walk alone at night in that deserted place, hearing footsteps, and shuttered conversations behind hair-line cracks of light; it was creepy.

Kitty sleeps in her string-sided cot. Jasper and Amaryllis slip to Harry's Bar for a drink.

Peter and Colin treat me to initial shyness. They are polite and prim.

Peter and Colin are mauling me, they are sitting on top of me, they are squeezing me through the gap between the twin beds. They are tipping Jasper's bed – judging by the pyjamas – upsidedown.

A fine old time we are having. They make a racket.

The bed has to be restored to its former shape and position, its mattress fitted on, its clothes disentangled and spread, the pillow puffed. The lights flash, off and on.

The lights are completely extinguished.

I think it must be a fuse gone.

Peter gropes towards the window, he knows where it is, and the furniture, but without my having to ask him. He opens the net-curtained glass, and draws back the shutters, which are on the inside, and not locked.

The central heating has been grilling, and the cool air is welcome, with the glimmer cast by the lights from across the thin street.

I explain to Colin about fuses, and how the hotel would mend it soon. But the darkness is uninterrupted; and he begins to feel more apprehensive.

'Lavinia!' he says. 'We'll be electrocuted, won't we!'

I am sorry I mentioned fuses.

Colin now is worried that lightning is striking us. Peter is nicely scornful. Peter's utter composure is a relief. He is enjoying himself. I persuade Colin to climb into bed. I perch on his bed and, with my arm round his shoulders, hug him very slightly. Peter fumbles to the bathroom.

I gather he cannot decide which china object is the lavatory and which the bidet. I don't think it matters, for once.

But the resourceful child says, out of the pitch: 'The one that has water in it . . . must be the lavatory, I've put my fingers in.'

He returns from this sortie; and he has, while he was in that direction, opened the main door to the landing; and discovered candles on saucers. I don't fancy Heath Robinson flames.

It seems time is passing to no purpose.

I should not have chosen to be a strange babysitter,

15

with strange children, in a hotel, in a foreign city, in the dark. There we were. There we are.

I lean from the window until my tummy hurts.

Those familiar cloak-and-dagger Venetian footfalls, apparently people. I see no lights on our half of the street. It is more than a fuse. It is trickier.

I fervently hope the cot-slumberer doesn't waken.

Colin calls me to his bed, he wants me to stay beside him. I stay beside him. I try to keep us on an even keel.

Peter has sharp ears; he darts out; and disappears; I hear him talking along the corridor. Amaryllis, then Jasper, as they approach. I hear them and breathe a sigh.

It is a power cut. A slice of Venice dark. Venice in the throes of industrial unrest. Jasper and Amaryllis have been anxious for the children and me; unable to make speed through the black and unlit; though they followed the Grand Canal. I remember the dead ends but a trip from murky drowning.

Jasper is all for Peter, snatching some clothes. I ask if I may join them. I am not sure if Jasper hesitated. Colin protests, I reckon he has his mother. I bolt for my coat and my gloves. I am thrilled.

As we strode across the face of San Marco like clouds across the moon, I realised I was extraneous.

At the Molo, the moored gondole make creak-creak noises; we tread over the water; and stand on the slatted cat-walks. I think I sensed that Jasper would have preferred to have been alone with his son. I long to remain, timelessly, in this bizarre vision. Jasper indicates the pyjamas, trousers, and duffel-coat that Peter is dressed in; and makes a move to go.

The stillness. The emptiness is uncanny.

I feel stiff and peculiar walking beside Jasper. Our

16

steps ring in the Piazzetta, and touch a deeper note in the drawing room of Europe, in which, with not a soul but ourselves to see it, two rows of lights suddenly blaze, one – the fluorescent – a second behind the other; and all around us are those clutching, striking, pawing images, illuminated.

> Venice in a fog: no sky, no skyline, blank mouths for famous churches and palazzi, no surface to the lagoon, a few piles like sticks rising from blurry water; the acid hooting and sirening of the vaporetti; voices; hush; the clouds drifting through the campi, visibly; and hollow canals. Giving her, Venice, an altogether different perspective. The air, raw. The aeroplanes, grounded.

Herded up from various hotels; waiting forlornly – stamping our feet, blowing on our hands – for a motor coach to whisk us, in a vain, obstinate gesture, to the airport; loaded into a plane; taken for a taxi ride, past fuzzy runway beacons; spending much of the day in resignation, tourist solidarity, blankets of gloom; feeding on morsels of news. In the late afternoon a plane circled overhead; we could hear it roaring, until the roaring was fainter, and Venice was abandoned.

Disconcerting, to have been wound up to leave.

I stumbled into a coach with the foolish fantasy of a fourth night in Venice.

The hotel we are taken to is a plush, palm-potted job on the barbaric shores of the mainland.

The men fret and telephone and telegraph their offices. The women are bothered by Christmas looming;

turkeys to collect from the butcher. The fog will not lift for three days.

And we are to be fed. The food is nasty. In the bathroom, there is a notice that the water isn't fit to drink.

Like sheep, we sidle into the dining room to be allocated tables. Jasper, Amaryllis, the children, and I, are assumed, somehow, to be together – we are quite friendly – and a single unit. As 'the family', we are placed at a table on our own. I am secretly delighted.

Little Kitty cries *nice nice* and *more!* before she has finished her plateful. Jasper instantly scoops up a heaped spoon of his own, awful ravioli, and increases her helping out of all bounds of possibility of what she can eat, and she never does manage to eat it. I observe that the act of giving his daughter part of his, though futile, is of infinitely greater pleasure than the gratifying of his hunger which, despite the quality of the food, is obvious.

The child takes a drink of water, from a glass, and she bites the glass.

Her mouth has bits of glass in it, her lip is cut at the corner and bleeding, a trickle of blood runs from the corner of her mouth, and out of her mouth from her tongue. Kitty is crying blue murder, not without cause, from her fright and hurt. I shall not forget the looks of anguish and the waves of emotion passing across the faces of those parents, as they leap to wipe the glass from her mouth, and the fragments fall onto the stiff white napkin.

It was as if I never saw them again.

> And however inadequate the visit,
> however brief, Venice was not to be
> touched, no steps retraced, would be

18

left to float in the memory, like an
unblinking eye, looking upwards.

THE ACT OF DARKNESS

Mary, Mary, quite contrary
How doth thy garden grow?
With silver bells and cockle shells
And pretty maids all in a row

I know there is more than colour in my cheeks. 'Like one of those roses you cut and take straight into church,' someone's lovely Granny said, with a face like one of those roses herself.

I am told I shine, I radiate; I'm not sure I want to shine for everyone; some people are not the people I want to shine for. But too many have mentioned it for me to be unaware. It cannot be the sweetness of my nature.

It is the glow of celibacy, I expect; the bloom seen on the scrubbed cheeks of nuns and shining from their eyes; not all, just some nuns; it may be mistaken there as the symptoms of sublimation, holiness. It is not celibacy itself; it is the struggle with celibacy. And not all, not even all nuns, have the same struggle. If you catch that look on a nun's face, you may care to think: beneath her habit, her body, if it had the chance, would lust, and strongly, for it is an ordinary, earthly body; and behind the glowing purity is a mind that has denied itself carnal knowledge. Doubtless there are nuns, spinsters, widows and widowers, wives, husbands, monks, priests who do not have as much libidinous feeling to thwart. A nun, anyway, may sublimate her sexual drive in such great love of God that she rises from the ground and has to be pinned down by the hem of her cloth to the cold and sweaty stones by her sisters singing, kneeling in the quire.

I have not fucked for ten years.

It is a long time. For the whole of the middle of my life.

Ten: one, two, three, five, seven, ten. The first two years are bearable. After that, it feels strange. *Not* fucking is extraordinary, it is the reality and has begun to pall. The seeds of the joke about onions, and getting them.

I have this vague puzzle: that other people fuck, that things happen to them, instead of a blank apathy that is now mine, instead of things seeming to be about to happen and suddenly vanishing, chimerically.

I catch myself looking at people's lips; I calculate the history of those lips, in the hours preceding, the night before maybe; the lips are perhaps bruised, are sore from being bitten; I find my hand, palm outwards, covering my own mouth, as if shielding it from nips of jealousy.

It's with a feeling almost of horror that I realise I am not now and never shall be much loved of anyone, especially cared for.

I look at the withered spinsters, twenty years ahead of me, with a new and appalled understanding. Virginia Woolf understood, that loneliness which stretches out and hasn't yet come. Virginia Woolf died two months after I was born.

I am not precisely pitying myself. I am trying to gird my loins.

I am resisting, I want to revolt against being condemned to silence because my life is not valid; because there is a rule against squealing; against pitying oneself; the unthinkable sin.

Desperation can be very quelling. I am shrivelling; so

24

that I am less, I sense, than the air I displace with my body; there is a gap between me and my outer shell; no, it is all shrunk, there is a vacuum; and which surrounds me.

I am aware of becoming dulled, I am afraid of a lessening in intensity, of feeling less. Where do roses go when they fade, where do old roses.

I am quite frugal. Though I am closed in with cold, steel-stiff, and forbidding, more and more each day, week, month, year, don't think I don't ache for it. A word of tenderness, a gesture.

For once again, my expression to be transformed by fucking; for contentment, an hour or two; relief, peace, and tranquillity; not always to have to notice what odd demands life makes; to smell someone else on my skin; for ten minutes, to live on for the next ten years.

Or five minutes. A kiss. To burn in my memory. To remember in order to forget.

To have desire again, to want someone, melting like a snowman at the feet.

There have been moments, many moments, when I want so much to fuck that I can only curl up and lie still. And even my mouth: my lips hurt to kiss. A simple thing, a kiss.

For the sexual charge, the electricity, to run, even through sleeves.

I have woken with breasts swollen and sore, pulsing, the nipples desiccated and peeling; tumbling, falling from the body as it heaves itself to sit on the side of the bed, from lying spreadeagled, supine and confident.

I have woken sopping and swollen, with a devil to suppress between my legs, and with dismay. To the splatter of summer rain.

I have woken with my cunt crying out, lips throbbing

and puckering, and an empty thumb print pressed into the back of my ear.

It's rather like waking with one's arms outstretched, embracing thin air, an emotional rictus – so that after a while, waking has become the focal point of the day, the point on which the day is hinged, or unhinged.

I want stuffing for the mouth, a cock, a tongue, a rolled-up handkerchief.

A disembodied member: the remembrance of skin, the texture, the unexpected softness and silkiness of penis-skin. And then I imagine that between my legs, clutched in my muscles, at the entrance of my cunt, anywhere. Inside me. The desire is detached, is the sensation alone, is in that one location of my body.

I am half a mouth: the sheets cover half my mouth as I lie on my side; I feel a kiss on half my mouth; half of each lip, the top, the bottom, is alive; the other halves, killed by the white, winding sheet, are dead.

I am balanced on a scream.

Not to float, but to step boldly out of frame, to swim naked in a sea somewhere, to act upon the moment; someone fondles your breast, and you trot along like a little dog, after the tugging leash of inclination, the flow of feeling, assuming it has a clear, pictorial direction.

It is not that I fear being myself, it is nervousness of the self I shall be in five years, one year, ten minutes. I am husbanding my future self, the person who will reflect, who will have to sit on her life, upon memory; upon a tuffet of memory, eating the cud.

At the present, I am poised on a fulcrum, having to be mindful of future and past and I don't know if, one day, I shall feel relief or regret or not be bothered much either way. I don't know that I have ever really

. . . adequately . . . regretted.

I have a notice of ageing, a wrinkling in the skin between the breasts.

If Venice signifies ecstasy, if she may be acquired as a symbol, there should have been a Venice chapter in all our lives.

If I can look without flinching. I don't believe in atonement.

I turned to nature. To tracks in the snow. To things that lead somewhere. I love rivers, canals, streams, water which holds the mirror up. I love lakes. I imagine swimming very much. The clasp of water, of glittering liquid. I will squat in my imagination by a loch in the Highlands dabbling my toes and watching my own body as it breaks the ripples, stroking the glass face, into the sun or away from it, toward the motionless, invisible heron, stubbing my feet on a submerged tree trunk. I am anxious about drowning; I am out of reach of help, out of my depth; and the long-tailed tits twitter in the pine tree tops. I wait for the osprey which could change one's life but which never appears, forever a possible, and its absence.

I take to the stones; rocks and stones and running water; slabs of rock, flat, and sloping into a river bed; with worn surfaces, rutted and grooved. I have lain, my spine against them; my shoulders on heather, that springs, and bark, that scratches; and on snow, which dissolves.

It is not the wetness of water, is is the darting movement, the staying still, the hand passed through it as if it isn't there. As though it were not real.

I restrict my excitements: to the hedgepig's grunting in the garden; to insects rising on the warm air, transfigured into fluff; to the heat of the sun.

27

I feel like a Swede at the end of winter.

There is a difficulty in abandoning oneself – head held mutely up to blinding light, mild, feeble light – to nature. In searching the sun and the wind and water, hoping to find hands, fingers, lips and cocks.

But at least it isn't as food is, quite disgusting after a few years' solitude, a disintegrater in the mouth, putrefying before its time, furring the tongue: that loneliness is purely subjective, an illusion, a delusion of the taste buds; my gob is sour with the wrong juices for the meat, fruit, and drink.

I will breathe life into a cheek, I construct a human item, holding the flesh in the hand of my mind: first the colour; filling it with the correct white, pink, pale, and blush; fleshing . . . it out; and then the lying of it to the skin of a pony's neck, or a dog's flank, or a cow's, or a coarse-haired donkey's. I no longer relish the smell of dog.

I am aware of isolated parts of my body which have no feeling; they feel and feel not; such as the hair on my skin.

Or I feel nothing else but cunt, twitching like the nose of a rabbit; and that is all I feel, all I am; the rest is dead; not numb, simply physically not there.

An unfortunate ghost is left clutching her cunt instead of her head, under the arm; where is the expression on a severed head – in ether above the severed neck? – for assuredly such spectres have expressiveness. Can it be the cunt's lips curl into a grin. Smile, cockle, smile. Alas, poor cunt, I knew her well. Alack, O cockle, no teeth, no toothipegs.

In medieval vernacular cockle was a name for cunt.

And pilgrims wore cockleshells in their hats to show

the world that cunts were above them, out of sight and mind, and well away from their winkles.

To put winkle into cockle, cock into cunt, is such a *peculiar* thing, if you think about it; and I do think about it; for one part of a human body actually to be fitted inside another's. It's a stupendous notion.

Penis seems feminine; women should have penises, men cockles, raw and red and angry and gripping; the temper of our sexes.

There must have been an Anglo-Saxon word for clitoris, somehow forgotten down the ages; if cockle has got lost, why not mussel; the metaphor will do nicely. I am trying to invent a decent word for clitoris, the ungainliest in the Latin language.

But longing is not all nameless; it too has flesh, and skin, and stiffening; it is far more than the stiff cock.

The sharing, missing it.

Having a basic need for that, to share experience, which without it has little meaning; wanting to be looked at and to look with. There is a near-imperceptible singing in the voice, in the mind; it says, I am alive; it is vitality. A joyous humming. I lack it. I am not so fragile now, not so hurt; but I should dearly like to be able to say 'we', not everlastingly 'I'. However many years is it since I shared a bath or washed myself in someone else's bath water. I do long for the sense of someone moving around, breathing, occupying a space, not to be bumped into. Not anyone. I loathe having people here at night unless I am exceptionally easy with them. I am used to houses where visitors can be shut off and avoided.

I am not talking about visitors.

It is that which I don't understand: how it could have happened.

29

I reject, but cannot escape, the facts, that may have set me on my course. I suppose I am falling back into a predictable pattern of aspirations and emotions; and summoning these with words which have been in service before, the drudges: feeling as others have felt; longing as others have longed; needing what others still need, and have lacked. It's not that I object to being unoriginal, a common phenomenon, or that I mind being lost in the multitude, my individuality no price at all; but that there *is* no escape.

I dispensed with virginity in a house where Admiral Rodney had lived. In the front bedroom: if not upon his actual bed, surely on the spot where he slept; he was born further south, I believe. I was unconsciously fulfilling my lifelong connection – and obsession – with the sea.

Two sweet, gentle, innocent old maids symbolically awaited the departure of my swain, downstairs. There was no blood, no rupture, no pain. The sea was sparkling and green with phosphorus. I had spent my virginity bestriding ponies from early childhood. To spare my landladies, the deed was further done behind the timber dock and in various nooks and crannies.

And so I lived with a man for two and a half years – we have left the seaside and are in London – in a room horribly red like a cave. I didn't regret it; but I wish it hadn't been. It remains my sole experience of living with a lover, as opposed to a friend. It ended awkwardly, and unpleasantly, and it was my fault. He was older than I was.

I flew to Italy, on a wooden seat in a train. I fled. I had some money. I embraced promiscuity, in a lyrical, hilltop Umbrian city; bounded by a wall, with gates, and arches. I slept very high up stone stairs deeply indented with the passion of centuries; the house was fourteenth century; from my window the view was mostly medieval; and far below a boy I presently fucked faked antique furniture in his uncle's courtyard, dressed in a suit with a waistcoat, singing or whistling.

I learnt the language quickly. I seemed to be acquainted with every lissome male and, more importantly, with many nubile females who were as I was, from England. For the first time in my life I was popular and gregarious, at the centre of the action. I revelled in it. And it went rather to my head. There *was* a Venice chapter, if such frivolity is acceptable. I enjoyed myself.

Under gnarled olive trees, and the stars; against dark walls; in open fields; in copses; beside the lake, and once, in the lake; beside the river; in tiny cars; in hotels willing to be tipped the wink; in derelict peasants' cottages; in a grand country house; at parties; in a primitive country house; after dancing; after drinking; after lavish meals; on mattress and board, rug and bed; in a little ancient room down a narrow street, down steps: I fucked. And mildly procured other girls for fucking, for friends. The latter was a mere adjunct to the more absorbing business.

I was twenty-one. It must have done me the world of good.

And then America. Long sprigs of mint, elegant, elongated, spiky leaves, pent up, pressing against the face of the glass, and crushed by splinters, drowned and weighed under in whisky and ice. I have a softness for Americans, those creatures constructed of milk and oysters covered in green spinach and cooked in the shell who swallow Scotch for breakfast. There was only one American but I have been rendered permanently sentimental about them. I lived in New Orleans and worked as a kind

31

of private detective snooping on department store personnel. It was a horrid job. I saw a black funeral with a jazz band, and a little old lady playing the piano in a funny place called Preservation Hall. I rode a bicycle and half starved saving for my fare home. I ate one proper meal a week; a horse collapsed and died outside while I was eating; I was hungry and ate through the agony.

After a tortured two, or was it three, years, during which I had managed to cross and re-cross the Atlantic sixteen times – I worked my passage, I sailed, I went to sea in a big liner, I still have the defunct union card, I have been a member of altogether three trade unions – and he had come to Europe hardly fewer, he and I occasionally coinciding in the same country at the same moment with often a divide of hundreds of miles; after I had stayed two months with friends in Hollywood – that was at the beginning; and after living finally in New Orleans, I withdrew; from America, to Africa. A journey that proved in the end to have been a decisive turning-point, with an Italian ship's captain of dark and brooding complexion, and with whom I went to bed.

There were more, there is more, a little more: but the rest is silence.

I was a woman whom no one had asked to marry.

Mary Swainson knew her at once. As a child she had been very much in awe of her. She reminded herself that she was now grown up and was going to marry Jack, the woodman, as soon as she thought fit, while Miss Turner, poor old thing, had never married at all. Crossing the road, to go through the coppice down to her boat, she smiled at Miss Turner with a queer mixture of kindness, pity and fear.

Then my mother fell ill, and though she recovered, gallantly, to some extent, I imagined I was needed, and I dug in at home, with a sense that there was nothing else I wanted to do. I wasn't needed non-stop, but I couldn't go and come as I pleased, because I surrounded us with animals. I had responsibilities.

If you are told someone has between six months and two years, at the most two years, to live, there is absolutely nothing else you want to do but stay with that someone you very much love. And if she has a terrific will and the energy to live, and lives not for two years but for seven, you still stay, gritting your teeth, in a paradox of emotions, and with faint, conflicting hope. You are not a sacrifice, the only alternative does not rest in you alone. You are free. It is nobody's fault but your own if you are mouldering. That is how it was for me.

I thought I could resume. It was stupid. A lot of water had gone churning through the mill. I was older. I hadn't the slightest inclination to sally forth metaphorically and look for a fuck as if I had been twenty-one again. I didn't fancy anyone I met, well, hardly anyone. Something had happened to me. I was changed, reclusive, and I daresay unlucky.

Unwanted attentions became the unkindest rub of all, the awful irony. It seems I have been the object of love, or passion, or of both. But I am not so generous I can give myself, my body, to the imagination of other people, unless the tune is called by me. People who have wanted to possess me; to pour their love upon me, except that it feels like piss warm from a chamber pot; to consume me, to ooze unsolicited love upon me; and as if trailing a scent, or a slime like a snail, to sit upon my sofa, breathing and expanding their souls in my own precious space, speaking words I don't want to hear, writing letters with words that simmer in the mind, forcing replies I hurt them by making; it is all too much. I long for a real love, and they sting me with their desire. I cannot be as gentle as I should wish.

I have a neighbour who sweetly offers. I am not tempted. He calls me Lavvy, in the face of hints and pleas, which castrates the notion. I appreciate the gesture. He has repeated the invitation with touching persistence on a weekly basis like hoovering the carpet for ages and ages: we hug each other. It's a habit. He claims he wouldn't be astonished if I succumbed. There is a convenient, uncomplicated cock, and I, I let sleeping dogs lie. Yet I catch myself wondering if I should. If, I think, I have done all my fucking, if I am never to as long as I live, won't I regret not taking the opportunity, no matter what? I feel better for the renunciation, for sticking to a principle. I should be substituting for something sad, something sadder. I observe my tepidness toward him. I dread being one of those females desperate to fit in their last stuffs before the candle flickers. And then I wonder if I'm making too much fuss, shouldn't I relax and take life as it occurs. But he's a nice next-door neighbour, with whom I have a comfortable, totally superficial relationship, and in common, nil.

Irrationally, I feel I can only expose my ten years of denial to a person I know intimately already, and whom I trust. I'm not suggesting it would show, in that I should appear unhandy – it would be as though I had fucked yesterday. It's quite different.

Something did happen to me, had happened to me. I discovered I couldn't come. It may sound idiotic: it shattered me.

I need to be able to explain to that mythical somebody. I can't pretend. I am not willing to fake orgasm. At that moment I am least ready to be dishonest.

It is humiliating.

It is mortifying.

It is all the more mortifying because for *years* I didn't realise. I thought sex so marvellous I couldn't imagine there was more. I must have known, yet I didn't. I was in that state of knowing and not knowing. On reflection, I can see that of course I knew. But I did not consciously either admit it or know that I knew. I skated over every indication which might have given me the hint. It would have been such an immense admission. I ignored it by turning my head the other way. If I hadn't been a reader . . . no, I read passionately and devotedly and have all my life. If I read books again, which I would have read then, it beats me, how I didn't comprehend. I discussed orgasm with men, without realising what I was discussing.

If someone asked me if I experienced orgasm, I answered yes.

It was confusing. There was the total unreliability of men, and even women, to describe female orgasm correctly, let alone adequately. It is with men I would have talked. I find women difficult; not for a long time have I grasped how friendships with women work, though I must have once. Sexual experience is empirical, and men, even women, tend to assert the general from the particular. That can be a little destructive.

I was ten or eleven when I borrowed a novel from the Boots's library in Ferndown - how different Boots's library books smelt, from public library books today, and how different they looked, with the metal hole in the base of the spine – which was French. The fact that it was French, I thought, explained a great deal. There were

35

descriptions of cock-sucking and cunt-licking so vivid I couldn't fail to understand precisely what those lovers – so very French – were employed upon. It was dark, and daring, and surprising, but it was clear. I remember nothing else about the book, except its smell; I think I was probably shocked; it must have been an 'unsuitable' book; but it has stood me in good stead. Female orgasm involves intangibles.

There wasn't, it seemed to me, when I couldn't avoid the problem, for someone who had no knowledge of the experience, any inkling of what to expect, any description, whether literary or from lovers' lips, which truly conveyed what it might be like. I felt I had been intensely stupid. I felt my stupidity increase.

I simply couldn't imagine what it could be like. I was misled and diverted in my search of such phrases as 'the little death', and to be 'in the clouds'; I seemed, principally, to be emotionally lacking, with those overtones of swoon; and I concentrated on the deficiencies of my mind. But to be transported by rapture is not really the mother and father, the sole kith, kin, and cousin of orgasm, is it? I'm not sure. It isn't, for me. Orgasm can be an orphan.

I was confused, too, by the non-fiction. A significant proportion of low-orgasmic women have lost their fathers early in life: well, sod that. The fears and failures of women, the ignorance, the reluctance to touch their own bodies, their partners' bodies, the taboos, the therapies, and theories; all that seemed nothing to do with me.

Nor had the men I had fucked with been ignorant, or hesitant, particularly selfish, or brutish, or insensitive. Far from it. It was tragic.

It was the Italian ship's captain who told me. You were made to fuck — born to fuck and be fucked, he said kindly, except in one respect. It *still* took a couple of years to sink into my soul. I treasured that remark like a drowning man clutching at a straw.

It seemed it was plastered abroad, on a placard hung from my neck, for all the world, a badge of shame: don't you bother with this frozen person.

Passion is not strictly the point, I thought it was. Passion is possible without orgasm, orgasm is possible without passion. I think if I had been male, I'd have felt castrated.

If you can't come, you are frigid; there is a name for your condition, and it is frigidity. No matter how else you are. The words blur my eyes with injustice, whilst outside the full lips of summer pout irritatingly.

A kind of outraged pride forbids me, ostrich-like, a dignified bird which nevertheless appears foolish, to try. It's as easy to make a fool of a woman as of a man.

I thought I should die without knowing. I wanted desperately, not to be denied another human experience. I withdrew into myself, nursing my secret.

I felt threatened by women in the tube: feminine, neatly painted and scented women, who would cry out at the moment of orgasm, that literary cliché which leaps from the page of every book as if to insult and torment me; like women in movies with contorted faces; and plain, unarresting women, ordinary women who were transformed by sex into writhing ecstasy; if them, why not me? I felt threatened by farmers' wives in country towns, and schoolgirls. As they palmed the hens' eggs and churned their butter and fed their ducks, or did their algebra, they too knew something I did not. They were possessed of the secret. They were real women who satisfied their menfolk, and theirselves. Abandoned females, or inhibited, ignorant, hesitant, passive females, they could all do it. Statistics didn't exist for me; I might as well have been the lone representative of fifty-one per cent of English women, British women, Anglo-Saxon women, for all I was aware.

That Italian bolstered my ego for the years to come. He made me into, for him, a fascinating problem. But at the same time, everything fell into place. I recalled the odd little rejections, the euphemistic questions, gentle probing. I remembered scraps of conversation and segments of the action, the context long gone, which had new relevance.

Nothing had ever so hurt me. Abstract thing.

I was chilled and bewildered.

One day, ripe in age, I picked up my electric toothbrush, touched with the smooth side my clitoris, and the trick was discovered. I was utterly astonished.

I had been reading, actually, an article in a feminist magazine about vibrators. I have never been able to bring myself to buy a vibrator; it's like having clean knickers on to be run over by a bus; what would people think if such an object was found in my flat when I deceased myself; nobody could suspect a toothbrush. I read this article and it came into my mind that in fiction over the years there had been mention, occasionally, of electric toothbrushes and in a spirit of curiosity I stuffed mine up me and got rather scratched; that couldn't be right. Luckily I persevered a second longer. I felt a faint shiver pass through my body.

I became obsessed for a while thereafter, and with practise felt somewhat more than a shiver.

I couldn't have believed it would be so physical. Indeed, with a toothbrush, it seemed entirely physical. It was something the body did, and it would do it though the mind was dwelling on cabbage and potatoes cooking for lunch, or the dog's dinner. It did it better if there was a large penis sticking up before my unseeing eyes, or if I had been thinking or reading erotically, but it didn't make all that much difference if there wasn't and I hadn't. It was completely automatic. How that was a relief!

All those men didn't not know about the clitoris; a poor fellow had pumped away at it so hard it was a pain. I had known since I was at school.

I have very little feeling in my clitoris — that dreary word again; in my oyster, my mussel; hence the expressions 'the world's your oyster', and 'the oyster of your eye'; almost none; and it is diminutive, heavily hooded. It may be a question of nerve-ends. It is, mine is, a useless organ; my feeling all is inside, or at the mouth of the cunt. I cannot come *by hand* for my life. I couldn't save my life if I had to, if I masturbated until kingdom come.

An unassailable, I think, fact. I wish it were not so.

If you examine the cockle, the shellfish cockle, nude and from its shell, you will see — I have been eating cockle kedgeree — the clitoris's likeness. Perhaps we have it all wrong, we have misinterpreted the medieval idiom. It fits, it fits; cock, and littel cock its female counterpart. Hey presto: cockle. Our forefathers had already plenty of nomers for the cunt. Is this cockle not cunt but the forgotten lost word?

That is why the shellfish cockle lacks mystery, mystique, and isn't the prettiest of them; the mussel opens its lips; so does the oyster; with force; a raw oyster on the

39

tongue is a taste incomparable to anything else on earth; and it is alive; it palpitates; seems to see you with its single lens; it swims down your throat, is not drowned in your gorge.

The cockleshells of the innocent-oh nursery rhyme could have been scallop shells, any fragile shell; but maids of honour were little tarts with curd filling.

A cockle is no pearl among shellfish, there are others finer and more fair, and more delicious. I want everything for my cunt, and I can't have it. In there would be and must be the sensation I crave, am mad for. The clitoris is fourth-rate, and the toothbrush routine is grotesque and pathetic; how else can I view it?

One might even call breasts whelks: what shape are whelks?

The toothbrush is white, slab-shaped, with room for a family of tiny brushes, black, red, blue, orange, and is made by Boots; the unfortunate Boot would not have liked his effect on my life; the predecessor was a Ronson, which had greater oscillation, a quality – like a horse – action; the Boots has a stronger motor, and is sturdier – the fat sleek cob of electric toothbrushes; its motor struggles on where other motors might fail; it is the peaky clitoris which has to move, rather than the brush as it would across teeth; it has a long life under trying circumstances, therefore.

I use an ordinary toothbrush for cleaning my teeth. Not from squeamishness. Not at all. To preserve the batteries.

The quaintness of the electric toothbrush renders it acceptable to the mind. It makes a noise like a tractor ploughing along the side of a hill.

In the beginning, narcissistic as a last extreme – what

40

else was there, though not much admiration involved – I would have had a bath. I had a habit then of shutting my eyes as if a painful image had appeared eidetically in front of me. I would scrape at my skin, and mould the muck from my nails into forms which I could destroy, and I was destroying myself. I would pull and tug at my pubic hair. I would stand and let the water run down me. I wrapped myself not in a towel but in my arms. I hugged myself. I was forced to. I would touch each shoulder, holding the knobs in my palms, cupping them. I was holding myself, the hands were mine, the hugger was me. I would be hot, grow cold; I turned my head away and when I looked back I was crying; my lips would ache, my whole mouth ached, first with wanting contact, to touch, to feel, to . . . yet not to devour, not to devour, I did not want to devour myself, I didn't want myself, by myself, at all.

I would lie naked on the bed. I rested my head on my hand; the hairs in the nape of my neck tickled and I thought of centipedes. The sun was shining into the room. It was a lovely summer, as this summer outside my window is. I watched vapour trails break across the sky, their pilots the nearest people to me as I prepared to drag my body from the depths, I thought, of being. I was wet. I was perpetually damp with tears or water. I was wet, I mean, from the bath. I would stroke my breasts, bones, pelvis, flesh. Tracing my wrinkles, the room's lines, ceiling, corners, walls, the light bulb hanging by a thread; curves of walnut, acanthus leaves, mother-of-pearl eyes in the handles of the chest-of-drawers; an oval mirror and columns of curtains; no breath of wind, no breath of anything; the room was part of me; was the red flesh; was the blue skin; in the sun was pale. I opened legs, lips,

41

eyelids, fingers, hooked up my knees . . . to overwhelm reluctance was like pulling on a long rope, or swimming underwater to a distant island; my blood throbbed and I thought I had lain all my life staring at the sky; as I picked up my funny, prosaic old toothbrush.

I don't bother with that kind of nonsense now. It is all a long time ago, and beyond me. It would seem quite foreign to me.

I learnt to place the soles of my feet together and to flatten my knees, which not only increases the intensity but made it even easier. I was a dog with a new trick.

I took my toothbrush away with me — what could be more natural — and had it off in the Little John Hotel in Hathersage, by pure coincidence. Hiding it under the bedclothes, hoping to muffle the genial roar.

I discovered, while it was still a novelty, that I needn't stop. I could come again, and again, and again, and again; once I was up, I seemed inexhaustible. Childishly, then, I attempted the obvious: to see how long I could go on in multiple orgasm. I had tried seven, three and seven being nice numbers. I lay down beside a clock one fine afternoon, when I trusted no one was listening — and if they were, they might think it was my hair dryer or that I was massaging my legs — and carefully counted; if muddled, I made myself discount one; it could have been more, it couldn't have been less; in two hours and ten minutes I had fifty-three orgasms; all good and thorough; I ceased from boredom and because I was a trifle tired; but thereafter I felt better equipped to face strange women in the tube. I held my head up straighter.

I would sometimes stuff a cylindrical bottle, plastic or glass, whatever I had of suitable size, into me, and by touching it, as well as the cockle, with the end of the brush, cause vibrations inside me. But inanimate objects are no substitute.

Those jokes to do with cucumbers and carrots are no more than that: *jokes*. Cruel jokes. The cold and damp of vegetables makes penetration impossible. The cunt shrinks as if confronted with poison. And I am not willing either to purchase or to cover a carrot with a condom.

I had long since turned the toothbrush over and allowed the bristles to grip me. It was as if my body had burst open; and the plastic bristles, they would be streaked with blood where they had bitten in. I wondered if I'd be scarred or calloused, but apparently not. I watched myself in a hand mirror in two ways; my eyes, and the sudden dilation of the pupils; and my cunt's mouth, inner lips, and the sudden spasm, the clenching of muscles, which was involuntary, as I pressed the switch.

I would listen to some music I didn't know, or at least wasn't familiar with, on the radio; and come with a climax of the music, a climax I didn't know precisely when to expect; without effort, with practise, with inspiration, as if the music were my partner and I was attending to its impulse and needs.

One evening, I was abruptly conscious of someone standing at the foot of the sofa, where I lay with my toothbrush, looking at me; since there was no visible person I assumed it was, not a ghost, but a human being out of the body. Whoever it was, with this person watching me, I reached a climax very speedily, and again, and again, immediately I pressed the switch, until I was too embarrassed, under the gaze of the unknown, to continue.

43

I rather hoped, with tongue in cheek, it wasn't my mother. But my mother was dead, and this seemed to be a living spirit. I am not given to such superstitions. The hair rose on my head.

It would begin at extremities, in my feet, in my hands, and shiver as if through my timbers, my veins and nerves; and my viscera would faint, like shrimps, or eggs; until its warmth collided in my groin. I was a spider with many legs. And depending on the amount of alcohol, hash, in the body, and water in the bladder; upon aspirins, music, sun, rain, storm and tempest, snow and hail, thunder, lightning, and the colour of life; of these, many alternatives; there may have been a fire in my head, in my groin; it may wash upon me slowly, or be abrupt, a disintegration.

If I remove the lyricism.

For up to half a minute, but usually for five, ten, fifteen seconds, there is a — still totally astonishing, absorbing — event in the body. There is a huge jump in the sensitivity of clitoris and cunt both, a stinging sensation, and sharp. The cunt muscles are convulsed by rapid, unstoppable contractions. The cunt, true to its mythological mouth and gullet role, gulps.

I do it for my health.

I think wistfully, from time to time, if only I could try my new-found knowledge with a live cock. I know in my heart of hearts it would be no use. I repeat, the men I have been to bed with were not inconsiderate, or thoughtless, or selfish, or stupid. No matter what ages we fucked for, or touched, no matter how gently, how agreeably I was led on, I doubt if I could come. I am *medically* frigid. It's as if I have learnt two entirely separate responses; and fucking is a very distant relation to masturbation with a toothbrush. I should much, much rather fuck. But I need to come. And never the twain shall meet. The two activities seem as remote from each other as cutting one's nails and . . . cleaning one's teeth. I should like to find out if the cunt can go it alone, but to do that I should have to commit myself to more than a toothbrush.

I am attuned emotionally to the explosiveness of sex, of male sex. I love that, to be whipped up, and to whip up, quickly.

I mind, I mind dreadfully; of course I do; I don't reckon anyone can take that away from me; it would be like trying to deny grief for someone dead; it is as precious to me; as real; as valid.

I meanwhile have to listen in my concrete tower to the simulating moans of the female below, or register the wild orgasmic shriek emanating at midnight hours from the elderly girlfriend in the house next-door, the genuine article I feel sure, and when I spot them holding hands in twin deck-chairs on the lawn I remember how she sounded like a hyena being tickled to distraction, and I pour a drop of affection for her out of my kitchen spy-hole; later in the year I miss her for him, she was so spectacular.

I want orgasm for my cunt, I do, I want it to arise from there; instead of the sense of something being missing, vacant; I want to be filled and then have an organ, a member, to grip onto, to flex myself onto without being able to help it.

I am bound to mind. To begin to feel otherwise, I should have to have a tangible feedback, a lover, and loving. Day after day after day.

To restore me.

In dreams and fantasies I want cocks in my mouth. In Italy the slang expression *una madonna,* of all things, describes the act of cock-loving in the mouth. I have always liked it. A taste: where words are failing me, are they not? But who the hell am I talking to anyway?

CUCKOO

Hail Mary!
Ich am sary
Haf pité of me and mercy
My levedy
To thee I cry
For my sinnés dred am I
When I thenk that I shal by
That I haf mis y-don
In word, in work, in thoght folý
Levedy, her my bon

dere Lady, prays he on his knees before the rood, make me whole! I know it is selfish. Give me back my life.

Robin Hood is 'civilly dead', *civiliter mortuus*, he is outlawed, outside the law, without its protection. His goods may be taken, he owns nothing. His land, if he has any, is his no longer. If caught in a crime and brought to court, he cannot plead his defence. If accused of trespass, he has trespassed. If accused of stealing, he has stolen. If he has eaten venison from the forest, or gathers more wood than by hook or crook he could, he has raped the vert and felled more than fifteen trees. If another man has his wife, if he had a wife, justice is done in heaven. He has no rights, not even the right to a life; he may be killed with impunity. He is a non-person. It is as if he did not exist.

Therein a metaphor of myself.

It is not easy to write, or think, directly. It is more acceptable to breed and rear opposites. If my feet were too big, I should pretend they were too little; if my steps were lagging, I should be lightly tripping. A deformity is concealed in a different deformity; a desire in a different desire.

Metaphor is neat, and pleasing. For an outsider of a certain kind, another outsider; for a woman, a man; all is interchangeable. Hope, failure, emotion. The last particularly.

49

I can be Robin Hood, or his doppelgänger Hobbe-hode, at any moment of the day: pausing, I raise my eyes, and am in the fourteenth century. It's a version of gallop-ing horses along verges and beside railway trains. On my sixth birthday, we had a fancy dress party: no marks for guessing who I was.

But can I project my consciousness, and obtain a result which is remotely close to the truth? I not only have to shed modern man, I have to regain another life, another landscape, quite another sensibility; with certain awarenesses stopped, like earths; and others – new, exposures – open. Why should I wish to?

Curiosity. No, day-dreaming. The better my friend in all likelihood never existed, except in the fourteenth century imagination. Robin Hood was a starting point, a fellow to invent upon; yet it's equally possible a lot of him has been lost; that his ballads are the thick end of the wedge; and what we have left is a mush of wooden splinters after a sledge hammer has performed. There is no mention of Marian, the tedious maid, in any of the early ballads; she probably came from France, the dar-ling and fault of morris dancers and troubadours, who immortalised her on May Day. And Robin Hood's repu-tation for robbing the rich to give to the poor seems a grave distortion of what he actually did.

The act of my imagination lies in isolated moments of perception. I think I see as he sees. I think I see the thing he sees. I latch onto time-stilled, fragmented parts of a picture; a single leaf, a twig, a branch gnawed by a squir-rel, not the tree; I have been brought up in an age of movie cameras; I can focus; I can zoom in; I can retreat, and telescope my eyes. If I could look at the colours of the middle ages; a painted-in-many-colours England; a little

50

England; the west front of Wells Cathedral bright as a rainbow, *painted*: but do I see red as he sees it; there are more reds in my spectrum than in his; he had an extra colour red, which he calls russet, and which to me is defunct; I don't notice russet anywhere at all.

Robin Hood was born at Little Haggas Croft in the parish of Loxley, the other side of Sheffield from his happy hunting grounds – of Sherwood, a royal forest, by Nottingham, and Barnsdale, north of Doncaster, which latter not being a royal forest was not under forest laws. It isn't the least inconceivable that he could have been in both places at once, and that each owns the same legend; he would have slipped from whichever was too hot for him; and from Sherwood to Barnsdale can't have been reckoned a great distance. It isn't far. A Roman road, Ermine Street, was the principal route north, and ran through Barnsdale; he called it Watling Street. He wore lincoln green in the summer, brown cloth in winter, like an animal of the forest, he changed his coat for seasonal camouflage. He imagines himself arrayed in scarlet, his merry many in green, because scarlet cloth is the most expensive, followed by green, then the humblest brown. He was born sometime before the turn of the century, living his own myth in the first quarter of the fourteenth century. A Robin Hood did live when King Richard went to Palestine and his brother John held Nottingham Castle, but that was not he. There were several Robin Hoods; either that, or none at all.

I say the ballads are his own invention. He pretends he has a company of comrades. He pretends he has company. He is so lonely he makes up stories and so child-like he invents his companions.

He was lonely in the outlawry he brought upon himself

51

by slaying a man he quarrelled with while ploughing; he was lonely in the shining forest.

He invents his most boon companion, Little John, also known as John Naylor, buried at Hathersage in Derbyshire; a giant skeleton, well over seven foot, and a tall longbow, were disinterred from the graveyard.

He invents Will Scarlet, whose name is a corruption of Scathelock; meaning, a fellow with a lock of white hair grown out of a head wound. In the ballads, Scathelock became Scarlock, and presently Scarlet.

He invents the curtal friar who tucked his habit into his belt, and minded the vegetable patch at his abbey of Fountains. He invents Allen-a-Dale, and George-a-Green the pinder of Wakefield, and Will Stutely, William of Gainsborough, and Right-hitting Brand. He doesn't invent a sheriff of Nottingham, exactly; there were dozens, and only two died in office. He hasn't invented anyone by the name of Marian.

His heroine is, and was, in a sense, his 'dere Lady', the recipient of much medieval adoration, a pin-up of purity. If it were not for Adam's fall, the Virgin Mary would never have been, neither the mother of God nor heaven's queen.

But the merry men were a figment of his imagination; life is otherwise insupportable. He can sublimate his emotions in love of our Lady; man cannot live by bread alone; which is not to believe he can live without bread; a nice bit of dough.

He dreams his adventures, with some touching self-deprecation. He fights, and is vanquished, and his former adversaries enter his dream-world.

He fights Little John on a bridge, John has a staff, Robin a piece of wood, John topples Robin into the wet.

Adam lay y-bounden
  Bounden in a bond
Four thousand winter
  Thought he not to long
And al was for an appel
  An appel that he took
As clerkes finden written
  In here book

Ne hadde the appel take been
  The appel take been
Ne hadde never our Lady
  A been hevene-queen
Blessed be the time
  That appel take was!
Therfore we moun singen
  Deo Gracias!

He has a pantomime struggle with Friar Tuck, he carries him across a river, and Tuck carries him; Tuck's bandogs catch the arrows which Robin's men loose, racing over the lee; Robin fights the friar with sword and buckler and is beaten, whereupon Tuck is offered and accepts Robin's fee and, as it happens, immortality of a kind he mightn't have contemplated in the abbey.

His characters, his friends, are potters, tanners, of an independent turn of mind. Robin detests the corrupt authority of church and town and state; he mocks and vilifies fat abbots and cellarers, smug priests, and frightens prelates. He loves our Lady, but robs her bishops; he loves his King, Edward the Second, but steals his royal deer. Of paradox, there is delight. He loves his merry men, a hundred in the telling, for he exaggerates. He loves the gentil knight, Sir Richard atte Lee.

He doesn't rob the rich to give to the poor; with small exception he robs the rich. He once gave something to an old woman whose clothes he borrowed. He robbed the clergy, the church, not merely for fun, but to pay his men and to clothe them.

The monasteries owned sheep. The land in Yorkshire, Derbyshire, and Nottinghamshire, was devoted to vast flocks of clerical sheep. Sheep and wool-farming were a profitable innovation.

He was pleased to be cruel. That has been glossed over. He was generous and kind when it suited him; when it did not, he took out his knife and carved the face of wicked Sir Guy of Gisborne, and Sir Guy's mother would not have recognised the corpus. He likes children. He loves silly, witty pranks. He sits discomforted bishops to face their horses' rumps, hands them tails for reins, thwacks the nags, and they are cantered home helplessly, tied on and in undergarments. He will have divested them of their silver too. He asks them how much they carry, they always answer none, or a miniscule sum; Little John tips it from their cloak-linings onto the mouldy.

The sheriff of the county of Nottingham – not the town – had at that time jurisdiction over South Yorkshire, a curious fact which accounts for that worthy's chasing Robin Hood across a sizeable chunk of England.

Robin Hood occasionally played at being Hobbehode, a mask, a shadow in darkness; the shy, the introvert, the recluse: Hob, a nickname for Robin; Hob the hood; a hood is the medieval word for disguise; hence, Robin and his hoodlums, muttered the Nottingham townsfolk, half-admiringly. Robin invents a disguise-name for Little John: Reynald Grenelefe, or from-the-greenwood. Reynald Grenelefe infiltrates into the service of the sheriff of Nottingham by posing as Sir Richard atte Lee's man, and leaves it accompanied by the sheriff's cook, who is ripe for life beyond the linden groves. The wife of Sir Richard atte Lee had actually, when it was needful, saddled a palfrey and galloped full tilt into the greenwood, land of fairies, land of Robin Goodfellow, heart of romance, where the last wolves still roamed, to find Robin Hood at his trysting place, a greenwood tree, which rhymes excellently with his merry men and he, and beg him rescue her lord, who was in difficulties because of helping the outlaw.

The word gallop was not in use in the early fourteenth century; people would have said 'to wallop'; and they walloped about on their horses; we retain wallop for an ancillary action. That is what Sir Richard atte Lee's wife would have done, walloped as fast as she could, or as fast as her palfrey could, into the forest. Wallopy wallopy.

For to tell Robin the sheriff had caught her husband strolling by the river. Robin is obsessed with rivers.

Robin is very fond of women, he adores some women; he sees them as a man sees a woman. I am not good at women, I am used to communicating with men, some men; when I am talking to a woman, I don't know where to look, since I look expecting to see a man; it was different with my mother, and with a handful of the creatures.

He keeps a hollow tree for his game. He has meat in such plenty the hollow tree resembles a butcher's; with a hundred men's stomachs to stuff, it resembles a butchers' row; so that tree, whose old roots are moistened by blood dripping, is named the shambles.

Women shouldn't open doors with babies at their blue and white breasts; babies shouldn't stop sucking, lifting their heads to stare at strangers; nipples shouldn't crinkle wetly and shine, together with the yellow light, through the doors; light shouldn't pour out into the rain, and the man, Robin Hood, outlaw, shouldn't keep stumbling back into the darkness; again and again he falls, while her skirts sweep the floor like a shooing broom.

Lythe and listen, all you that be of freebore blood, how Robin Hood lost his heart and cock for a brief spell to Hilda, the wife of the gentil knight, Sir Richard atte Lee.

It was in the heaviness of summer; a weight, which is familiar, and much loved; and languid, it rests like a body upon one: he had marched already in the year past primroses, wild daffodils, wood anemones, he had plucked the bluebells which wilted and swayed at the neck and oozed their sticky life from the stem; he had wandered by fields of rape, scenting their honey; he had watched the new, pale beech leaves strengthen and

56

mature, and the seedlings and saplings reach for light or bend into cripples if they could not have it.

It was the turn of the barley, the poppy; the wheat and the tare, the beautiful weeds; the full hedgerow; the mouse and the weasel; the flown birds; of stag parties; and delicately snoozing hinds. The weather would be fickle, not constant; as an English summer weather ought to be.

An Englishman's home is his castle. The castle of Sir Richard atte Lee, the castle of the ballad, was no more, no less, than a stout hall, with bowers off, close to the midden and fumed with good cows and sows. In unusual, unanticipated circumstances – Sir Richard in Nottingham and sleeping overnight at the inn called *The Trip to Jerusalem,* the children at their grandmother's – Robin Hood visited this refuge, so empty and still. And Hilda invited Robin to eat a coddled egg.

——I do hear there is a way of cooking eggs stirred together. They are then scrambled. It is like poaching, without the water, when you break the yolks by mistake, I think.

Robin's larder was bare, and he was grateful; he hadn't the slightest intention of biding after he had eaten the egg, of doing anything but eat the egg and depart; Hilda had no ideas beyond the eggs.

He would not have dared touch Hilda. If she touched him by accident, he was shot through with lightning. That the gentil knight and his dame supped often on lightning pleased him.

Hilda coddled her own egg soft, his hard; men and women are thus with eggs. Hilda's eldest daughter, she said, was going through a stage of being plump.

——Puppy fat is important in a young girl's growing.

57

——Is it, Hilda, why?

——It must come to them in order that their breasts may largen; ladies with small breasts never had their puppy fat; when the puppy fat disappears, the breasts do not.

Women tend to want soft eggs, men tend to want hard: she supplied him with egg and spoon.

——Do gladly, Hilda said.

He thought, Hilda looks frightened. He caught a fleeting expression and it was oddly apprehensive. She has no need, he thought; I feel content to sit on this bench eating my coddled egg, I am not lustful; while she is eating hers.

——Isn't it manly to eat with a big spoon, she said, we have only these big spoons.

He didn't care a jot; he was accustomed to eating eggs in his fingers. The brown mead glowed; the butter on his toast was thick; he dipped his hand into the grapes which were covered in a pollen of bloom. He stared curiously at her.

——Will you have honey? From my pet hive.

——How many swarms have you this year? He nodded thanks.

——Bees are clever, she said.

——I take your strays, maybe, he said.

——Don't you get terribly stung, climbing for them.

——Of course, he said.

The dogs were barking.

——I could never live with any other man, Hilda said.

——No, he said. He thought, I wouldn't want you to, what a peculiar thing to say. They shifted from kitchen to hall. Hilda sewed peacefully, and sang. Tears rose in Robin Hood's eyes without reason. He knew Hilda had seen he was crying, but he made no sign of it, simply let the tears drop out of his eyes, and soon they stopped of

58

Sumer is y-cumen in
  Ludè sing, cuccu!
Groweth sed and bloweth med
  And springth the wudè nu

  Sing cuccu!
Awè bleteth after lamb
  Lowth after calvè cu
Bulluc sterteth, bucke ferteth
  Meriè sing, cuccu!
  Cuccu, cuccu
Wel singès thu, cuccu
Ne swik thu never nu!

Sing cuccu, nu! Sing, cuccu!
Sing cuccu! Sing, cuccu, nu!

their own accord. Hilda showed him some of her most precious possessions, bringing them to him one by one. He knew she didn't understand how he was outside and incapable of living an ordinary life; he wished she would understand but he didn't expect it of her.

Robin Hood sat on the floor because he was uneasy on chairs. He didn't remember the move from chair to floor, he seated himself on the rushes by instinct. From there he said:

——I must go. Although he didn't budge a muscle.

Hilda doused three candles and spread her skirt beside him; he would have been very surprised if he had not swallowed several jugs of mead and had she not also. She sat near him, and hugged his crooked knee.

——You are warm, he said.

Robin Hood accepted, somewhat mistily, that he and the lady Hilda were down amongst the hounds; he was without his head, without thinking; he held her body, and he kissed her; then they both lay – were lying – on the floor; her clothes appeared to billow about them, wrapping them in clouds. He thought no further than kissing her, and her kissing him; he was alive, nothing else; having been kissing on the floor he expected he would leave. And so when Hilda said:

——Let us go to our bed, it's hard on the floor . . .

Robin Hood was astonished. Their bed: he felt he would have hated her if she had dissembled; he felt this fiercely through all the wine he had drunk.

——I have to piss, he said.

——And I, she said.

——You first.

They went to the closet, the dry privy.

——I can't, said Hilda, squatting soundless, with a

60

nervous giggle.

After he had pissed she clasped him and propelled him gently forward, her arm was around him. I oughtn't to, he was thinking feebly; I desire her so much, I cannot deny me her.

He subsided with her onto a bed which gave under them, in a stupor; their legs dangled over the edge. Hilda slithered her hand into his braes, and without more ado, she gripped his prick; she fingered him, and when she had explored him from tip to toe, she cuddled his balls.

——Shall we climb beneath the blanket, he said.

He remembered having thought, if we were to fuck, I should want to get into a bed with her, both of us naked.

As they stood they bumped, they collided, and reeled to corners of the chamber. He was aware of her tipping her long garments over her hair; and of her shrewd glance, seeing and unseeing, at his naked body.

They met again in the middle of the bed. Robin Hood felt he'd been tumbling into bed with Hilda for all his life; she fitted exactly with his previous idea of her; there was no separation of the reality from the dream. Familiar, and not familiar. He clung to her.

——Your heart, he said. It was thudding against his body.

The linen was cleaner and crisper and cooler than any he had lain in; the mattress was softer than any he had known. Her waist-length hair was in his mouth.

He was shy; he didn't touch her cunt. He half-knelt beside her, and his cock was on her breast. He stretched his legs on hers, beside hers; she put her hand on his cock. They rolled over, so he was at her other side, and all the time they held each other in their arms, and kissed each other, with the most simple, child-like pleasure.

When he came to put his winkle in, she took hold of it.

61

A hair lay across the entrance to her cunt. He shoved his winkle in, notwithstanding the hair, and paused, as if to take stock. He drew and moved his cock in her cunt and she in her excitement brought her bent legs up to his ribs, and so that he was hugged by her thighs.

——Your thighs! he said.

She let her legs fall. She made tiny noises, they escaped her lips. She flattened her legs and he gathered them up with his knees. She was smiling. He knew it, he could feel her face.

Hilda's hands were in his hair, on his back, on his bottom, on his arms. Robin was almost overwhelmed, he burst with such an intense tenderness; he felt very friendly, and fond of her.

He hid his mouth in her neck. I wanted to know her, to fuck her, to clamber over her in all directions, he thought. Hilda struggled, her belly leapt at him.

——I fuck thee, he said. Hilda laughed aloud. Her cunt was convulsed with laughter. His winkle poured seed into her limp body. She held onto him as if she'd never let go.

——Shall I stay inside you? he said.

——Yes, said Hilda baldly.

——I've taken advantage of you, he cried.

——I've taken advantage of you, she replied. And I shall leak into our bed, she added, muffled.

——Why? he said.

——No control, she said. He guffawed.

Then Hilda slept. Robin lay half over her, with his face in the goosefeather pillow, her hair spread there like a quilt. Her breast rose, and sank on a breath. She breathed so quietly he felt new amazement. They remained motionless.

I have a gentil cok
  Croweth me day
He doth me risen erly
  My matins for to say

I have a gentil cok
  Comen he is of gret
His comb is of red corèl
  His tail is of jet

I have a gentil cok
  Comen he is of kinde
His comb is of red corèl
  His tail is of inde

His leggès been of asur
  So gentil and so smale
His sporès arn of silver white
  Into the wortèwale

His eynen arn of cristal
  Loken al in aumber
And every night he percheth him
  In myn ladyes chaumber

When he took his crumpled winkle out of her, she sighed. It was the sound, to him, of a breeze dying, the groan of a branch that will crack, in sadness. She slept the sleep of tiredness. He lay with his arm across her belly, facing downwards by her side. He brought his arm back. He turned over and opened his eyes at the rafters. He wondered what on earth he was doing in that lovely droopy bed, with Hilda, with the good smell and taste of love, of fucking; he was dreaming, but he felt so comforted and real he didn't bother to pinch himself.

He could not sleep. Try as he would. He discovered soon he could not breathe. He was used to the open air and he was stifled. The window, where there was a slit of grey light, seemed unnaturally distant. He threw the coverlet from his body, and was oddly chilled, and still he couldn't breathe. He fought for air. He ached for the window to come nearer. Hilda had dragged the bed-linen into her arms, she was apart from him; he considered nestling up to her bare back and bottom, touching her, but she seemed to be making, with the angles of her spine and legs and head, a gesture of farewell, which he had to respect.

He had been terribly contented.

He longed to leave her, abandon her, to be out of doors, to find himself, in his own place.

Hilda straightaway turned, and her face was close to his eye, and lip. It was hours since fucking. He was thankful she had awoken. He spoke:
——Shall I leave you?
and he realised she wasn't awake at all, she was fast asleep, or she didn't remember whom she lay a-bed with; she gave no sign of recognition, she answered unintelligibly and turned back, taking the quilt. He was cold.

He moved, to get out from the bed. Hilda threw herself suddenly face upwards, in the gloom, and said:
——What are you doing?
——Putting on my clothes, he said.
——No! she cried. No, don't!
——Yes, he said.
——Have you slept?
——A little, he lied.
——Oh don't go, she cried once more.
——I would fain, he said awkwardly.

He held his braes to the light to see how to draw them on. Her eyes followed him. She lay on her back at the side of the bed which was nearest him. It was not her usual side, he knew without question. He was in no mood to question anything.

He searched for a shoe. He couldn't find it. She said:
——Light a candle.
——I shall have to, he said.

When he had lit the candle, and found the shoe, he saw she was looking at him. He felt tousled. Her cheeks were flushed from their loving.

He quenched the flame.

He sat on the bed. He would have kissed her, he hoped she'd kiss him; but she didn't, she stared at the rafters, far from him. He thought sadly, *she regrets it,* she would rather it hadn't happened. He put his head on her breast, in submission. Her shoulders, her arms, her throat, her breast, were covered in a dew of sweat.
——Bye bye, he said.

As he slipped from the castle, the castle door caught in the wind and slammed shut with undue force. But he was laughing, he couldn't help laughing to himself, as he left, and went into the night so fresh and alive.

Robin Hood plunged into the lefes grene, and heard the foulys sing their dawn song. He bolted like a horse, not caring how thick the undergrowth, nor how prickly the brambles; whether he knew his path, or had lost it: his feet were sodden from the ditches he had stept into with shuddering jolts. It was summer, was it not. He was filled, consummated, with well-being. He put his fingers into foxglove-cunts. He sprang the shooting hazels. Thwacked them.

In his shirt, on his skin, on his arms, the scent of her lingered; her particular, individual smell which delighted him; he snuffed it in, for days and days, without washing, until it finally died away.

His shoulder was bruised; his flesh had red dapples; he noticed it with mild surprise; he had no recollection of her teeth and tongue; he couldn't remember her hurting him: then he did remember. He was too experienced in clandestine love to have blemished her.

He did not attempt to return. He knew that was right. Like a hawk he waited, his senses suspended, to drop out of the heaven on top of her; though never to maim, or kill, least of all to carry her off in his talons; to fuck her, to fuck her.

Later he retreated into the heart of the forest, to the dark oak trees, where he might nurse his pride.

Because:

——Nay, Hilda said, nay, my duck. Twouldn't be good for thee.

Not good for me? he gasped inwardly. The irony of it hit him hard. He did not, he trusted, betray himself by as much as a murmur.

——You were kind to me, he said.

——It is better, she said.

66

He was hurt. A smile dawned, and he laughed.

A child of Hilda's had scarlet fever, and the rash spread; the child was fretty. Hilda seemed half-estranged; whatever Robin said somehow was wrong; if he was miserable for the seriousness of the scarlet fever, she would declare it nothing more than a bad cold, when it was obvious it was awful; and having scorned him, she would the very next hour speak of her misery of the fever, so he was quite nonplussed.

He blamed himself; his mind was embroiled in a tussle of its own; his mood was with mercury; he struggled to maintain a recognisable self for her; yet he was for ever thrown by her; cast into a tremble; he was afraid of wounding her in a way he couldn't understand; she required him to be a whole person, in spite of her striking out at him; he was nervous of being cut down.

He stopped wanting her, at least on the surface, because she stopped wanting him. He responded to her desire, and if it waned, so did his. It distressed him. He burnt desire to live. It was the wanting which counted. To fuck is lovely, but to be desired, and especially to desire, is to him a source of life. It was as if he starved, was parched, and grew weaker.

It seemed to Robin Hood that he regretted his flight from Hilda's body, before daybreak, when he could have stayed all night long, and fucked her again in the morning, more than anything in his life. He knew she was not for his loving, he had never believed otherwise. He had not dared love her. But how wistfully he thought of her; he felt tantalised; he had a feeling of having left something unfinished.

67

OWL

R   Alas, the silver bells were censers, the cock-
o   leshells monks and prelates, the pretty maids
b   nuns. It was but a dig at the garden of Catholic
i   Mary.
n   I interpret illusions.
l   At Torcello, it is God, the Christ-child, who
e   carries salvation, in the form of a scroll,
n   symbolising the word. Or
d   nobody carries salvation. I
to me thy bow   perceived a medieval, sacred
                pun. MARIA, PORTA SALUTIS,
MARIS ASTRUM, sea star, salvation's door; by her Son, sets
free those whom Eve had made sinful.* Her single
trembling tear speaks quicker than the word of God.
    The silence of winter. The owl and the hoar-frost.
Breath suspended like disbelief in the air. The trees
slumber so deeply during the night he feels they may be
dying. He sees the faces of his imaginary friends drop
and glide away. His hands shake. He has chilblains. His
arrows fall short, or fly wide, too high, too low, or break.
The arrow shafts snap. They shiver with their heads in
the brittle grass. Whistling in the wind, derisively. They
are lost. He can do nothing. He can do nothing right. It

*FORMULA VIRTUTIS MARIS ASTRUM · PORTA SALUTIS PROLE MARIA
LEVAT · QUAS CONIUNGE SUBDIDIT EVA

71

doesn't work, whatever it is.

In my mind's eye an arm, which fades at the elbow, a light tan colour, fair-haired; the fist, the fingers, arrow-making; I know the weight of the pile, I have stroked the belly of the fletched arrow, the nock, the sliced feather; the grey goose who flew with those pinions left her scent, long gone, at the root, plucked fresh.

No more the crumbling of the brown-bread earth, for it is frozen hard; but the light of the fire dancing on wet holly leaves, and the acrid smell of damp hoof parings. Nothing grows under a holly.

No more picking of blackberries in gentle rain; furry, bearded, and oozing juice; the blood and the juice trickling, running, staining, in self-injuring sensuality, when I alight on Robin Hood. No more warmth and love seething through his body, slackening fear and soothing hurt. But a sadness of never before. Not for any one person, nor for any one thing.

An anguish, like ether. No body left, no hands, no feet on the ground, nothing but invisible hurting, without a cry to be heard, the expression having departed, only its space remains.

A surface of cheerfulness, kept effortlessly, real, and not contrived, like the glitter of ice in sun and moonlight, day in and day out, nights eternal.

I light a bonfire, and every time I want to die. Old ladybirds crawl and flutter in the leaves, towards the flame, the heat.

Nothing grows under a holly. This is not the life I imagined for myself. I want to make sense of my life.

Its berries are yellow, not red. The beech leaves are ghosts, the twigs are bare. I used to chew beech leaves, as a child. I associate them with slimy, waxy pews; they came from the hedge which led to the school chapel.

The edge is taken off the day.

The heat of the fire made the leaves stir in the summer, the twigs and slenderer branches waved; and the haze shimmered. I discovered fire in the summer. But am a water creature, full of water images: I could return to die in water – or could I? I am helped by the sight of water; rivers and streams; canals; and drops of dew. The prismatic dew. On my table, in my room, is a prism: somewhere in the room, on the white walls, if the sun is out and shining at the correct angle, there will be an inch of brilliant, concentrated rainbow.

Bonfires: good fires, or bone fires; skin of smoke and sun; he presses the crook of thumb and forefinger against his lips, repeatedly, a childish habit; or the crook of his arm in his mouth.

The trouble was, he frequently *was* cold, even if a man who could relish the east wind chapping his face. He lies on his bow in the winter, to shield it from damp and frost; if the damp penetrates, and then the frost, without any warning, the bow could break. Very dangerous. He gives his bow his own warmth. He leans against the trunk of a tree to sap its strength.

I was well into my twenties before I could stand up straight and hold my shoulders back; my seat on a horse was little to admire.

The green and the blue have gone, sky and leaf; the pure speckled voice of the thrush, deep-throated, spreading his wings slightly, to sing, to make the breast bigger inside; and the male blackbird, with his darting run, marking his territory where the shadow of the great tree falls at noon.

Heart of oak, heart of lettuce, human hearts. A conceit. He doesn't notice when the oak, which held its leaves longest, lost them. He is eating his heart out. I am only gasping: water, water. Trench soldiering. The comforting hush of snow, the enclosing; the shutting down of the horizon; creating virgin soil, and virgin sounds.

The winter passage: send my roots rain.

the fine pleasure is not to do a thing but to feel that you could and the mortification that goes to the heart is to feel it is the power that fails you

For whatever it is you are given, it shall surely be taken away.

For whatever you will receive, it shall be removed.

You will lose it, too soon you will find it has left you, and gone.

Life, love, health, happiness, your heart's desire.

There are rodents skipping and twitching in the trees: the garden squirrels; the grey, plain, characterless, thin-tailed squirrels; they sit on the lawn, don't hibernate, are chased by cats. The garden is peopled by tree-rats, the forest by proper red squirrels. The forest moves further and further from the garden.

A chill wind blowing. Noises that are not noises, husbanded in the head; not feared; expected guests.

The artefacts of madness: a collection, a heap of cockle shells.

In Rome: the hand of the guide to the catacombs, tattooed with a small, blue, inky cross; the voluptuous air above; the palmtrees on the rooftops; my last abroad before my being a daughter at home.

I dreamt I heard the first cuckoo of spring, a cuckoo so real, so intense the experience, I can't believe it was a dream, yet it was, and must have been.

Dreams of an intensity which begin to suppress my

74

days. I sleep with my arms crossed, protecting myself. I become either drunk for sleep or in dread of it.

Birds who eat weed-seeds and make nests with thistledown: they hang flowers, forget-me-not, over the edge.

The feel of penis-skin, soft and silky. The sheen of a crow's back. Walking away from nature. Hardly aware when spring follows winter, summer spring; whether there are bluebells, or primroses, or turning leaves. Nothing grows, not in my house. I can see I drive animals crackers, bulbs blind. The seeds I sow, they sprout, and they blacken; only the ficus benjamina, the fig, the cunt-plant, seems imperturbable.

Oppression heavy: I try my hardest for settling snow, the snow that is kin to water, and an ecstatic image. Conspicuous alone, the limits of life have to be drawn in.

If I were to sleep beside a single person, thinks he, for many years, and hoped to sleep beside her for many years more, sleeping – dropping off to sleep, lying asleep, waking – by another person, once in a while, would be a curious and singular pleasure.

Is disguise the deception of self, or of others, or of both; of some yet not others, selective; of the characters in the play, not the audience; has one forced oneself to believe in one's own disguise?

> Whither shall I go from thy spirit? or
> whither shall I flee from thy presence?
>
> If I ascend up into heaven, thou *art*
> there: if I make my bed in hell, behold,
> thou *art there*.
>
> If I take the wings of the morning, *and*
> dwell in the uttermost parts of the sea;
>
> Even there shall thy hand lead me, and
> thy right hand shall hold me.

> If I say, Surely the darkness shall cover
> me; even the night shall be light about me.
>   Yea, the darkness hideth not from
> thee; but the night shineth as the day:
> the darkness and the light *are* both alike
> *to thee*.

The ecstasy of the writers of the bible. Church cunt.

I understand how killing takes on a changed complexion after the first time, once you have killed, and a leaden corpse lies on the ground, where you, still alive, are standing, and it was you, who caused death to happen. I understand perfectly, I know it would be easier. You have baptised your mind with blood, blood not necessarily running from the body, but congealing, clotting blood, that coursed in veins such as your own. There is nothing romantic about it.

I am the last person to be sentimental over animals.

I have sent all to their deaths — dogs, cats, horses, calves, fowls — with commonplace pangs.

I have loved many animals, I have had a passion for only one.

I possessed a dog, or was myself possessed by him, who was exceptional, surpassing all other dogs; and it is to his death I refer; the rest were . . . animals. I had to deal out his death, three years from the beginning, the whelping, when he chose me, nailed me to loving him, by crawling, before his eyes were open, long before, always to my feet.

A most peculiar phenomenon, death. And watching dying: a minute here, a minute there; life emptying and draining; flowing and ebbing; an archetype-image which has no real meaning until you have witnessed the original.

On a winter morning, out early, I rode past a very tiny

bird, a sparrow, which had been pinned in the road by a car tyre, its legs squashed into the asphalt. The neurotic four-year-old I was riding – well, when up on him, you didn't much want to climb down. I should have dismounted, and knocked the poor bird on the head; but I rode on, for no good reason. I remember stopping, and staring down at it, and its staring up at me, almost imploringly; and the silence; and the extraordinary way its legs were. I feel ashamed to this day.

And then that strange moment of unseeing, in which an accident can occur, even with utterly careful beings: when the signs are ignored; seen but not registered; as in human relationships; registering below the level of consciousness, the other's expression, tone of voice, the flickering, barely perceptible movement of eyes and hands and skin, and recalling them too late, made powerless – stung, neutralised – to respond as you should, and would have, had you known.

The sheep believed she was a donkey, and died, never realising she was a sheep. I reared her as a lamb on the bottle. I reared two. They trotted behind me into the paddock, I showed them the grass, and had to wait while they ate it. And after she had imprinted on me, after the ram lamb was returned to the flock to be made mutton, for duty at the abattoir – not for nought was his name Napoleon; she presently ceased to be Josephine and was simply the sheep – and after I had been forgotten, she evidently assumed she was, like her companion, a donkey; bustly and woolly, she stayed on with us, petrified of sheep: if the flock was milling up the lane, followed by the shepherd with his crook, a quaint sight, she fled as fast as her four legs carried her, baa-ing pathetically.

Just as one loves many human beings, and in a whole

77

lifetime two or three more than the rest, one loves many animals, and a single dog, or horse, or monkey, with a special love, most of all; and if that dog appears to love you more than any human has, or can . . . in terms of personality, presence, every other animal is, thereafter, a disappointment.

I should not have left the sheep, aged seven, in a field with, besides the donkey, a mischievous pony, who chased her, to the point where she tore through a barbed wire fence, or perhaps the pony bit her, or both. I should not have glanced so casually at her, nor considered she could come to no harm, in the adjacent paddock. Though I say it myself, it was rare for me to be negligent. I saw but did not see. I saw without registering, let alone thinking. Her chin was flat on the ground, her neck stretched along the cool earth. It was not the usual position for a sheep, but she did sometimes lie like that. Her expression was her customary one of long-suffering and indignation.

The blow-flies filled her sores and wounds with eggs, and I didn't approach her, not near enough. I should have parted her wool and seen she was sore and wounded. In her sweaty, suddenly unhealthy fleece, they laid her with maggots.

And there she festered, her maggots hatched, and started to eat her alive, which is the thing maggots do. A day . . . two days, I don't know, went by, until I saw, with a shock, she was giving up. I took notice.

She was old, she was over-fat. She and her maggots had to be heaved into the back of the car, she couldn't make the journey home on foot. She smelt: not of sheep tang, but of dying, of mortification.

With borrowed disinfectant, exceedingly strong and carbolicky, we tackled her together, my mother and I.

78

For nauseating hours, we held open the rotting wool, which fell off in our fingers, and the flaps of flesh. Underneath those flaps, whither they had gnawed, the worms wriggled and squirmed, in their thousands, great white clusters of them; and slowly, painstakingly, we found more, and more. She had to be tipped upsidedown when we finished on top. She was weak. She groaned. Her stick black legs stuck in the air. There were maggots in her elbows, like bunches of pale, shifting grapes, and strewn liberally across the straggly, blackened wool of her belly and breast. She was sopping, and the vicious disinfectant must have burnt her. Then we surrendered also. We turned her onto her knees, and permitted her a breather. She lay in a shadow, against the corrugated, in the shed behind the nettles, rasping.

I thought, she's had it. The neighbouring farmer pronounced that it needs more to kill a sheep. I reckoned she'd be dead by morning, from bronchitis, or pneumonia, and shock.

I was right. I have an eye for it.

Dog or no dog, as far as I was concerned, I might as well have been murdering a human being, and I shall not be as awesome of killing, as I was, ever again. It altered me. It loosened a connection somewhere. Duty towards animals was often difficult and complicated.

It seemed that there was everlasting death in that other life I lived.

The elderly hens, their six bodies, five with heads attached, one separated from hers, its yellow beak, crinkly red comb, skull suffused in crimson, in a box behind the barn: out of practise, a man had pulled her head from her body, wringing their necks for me.

At the abattoir, a pig is screaming. Carcasses hang in

rows like trees in an avenue with their roots on giant meathooks. As each beast is forced in, it faces a steaming fellow, or a twitching thing on the floor. A pig is being scalded in a tub. A cow, belly agape, swings slightly, aloft. A dab hand, with pride in his work,, is slaughtering. In the pen an animal is watching. If they are pushed they have three lambs or two pigs in at the same time, which is illegal. The pig which is screaming ought to have been properly stunned, and insensible. The humane killer sits on the window sill, in regular use. The pig is stunned but not insensible. It is attempting to stand. It is thrashing around on the concrete and trying to find its feet. It seems to be looking directly at me, and asking for help. I am embarrassed. I am a visitor, halted between beef and mutton, the veal, the pork, the offal, the paunches on pegs, tripes and intestines. Tips of dirty hooves poke forlornly from a vat. The pig, who has been bungled, she goes on screaming, with her throat already slit – the knife cut not from ear to ear, but lengthways, hardly more than two inches – and the blood pulsing in vast prolixity, she screams until her scream is a gurgle. An unlucky gilt.

It is impossible to describe to someone who hasn't had the experience of the affection of an intelligent dog, how anxious he is for your well-being, how he senses your moods, and strains to breathe life into you.

If his notion of heaven plainly was to remain with me, if every muscle, every bone, every particle of his body precipitated love and adoration, if his mind pursued me relentlessly, and all this was indeed so, his devotion, that of a dog, had a value to me, of a depth no one could have perceived.

He knew, when I went away, how long I would be away, and began to expect me at the time of my return.

He had inherited the characteristics of his breed. He would grasp my wrist in his mouth, and hold it, leading me – painfully – through the door and into the house, moaning a welcome as well as he could with his mouth shut. He would sit himself down on sofas and chairs as a human sits. Ironically, he was the best trained and by a long chalk the most obedient dog I ever had. Summoned, he came at the gallop, immediately, narrowly missing knocking you over, and at such speed he couldn't stop, pelted on and had to catch you up from the opposite direction he'd arrived from. His body was larger and much heavier than mine. He was a handsome dog, a dark, red fawn, neatly put together. He was the pick of the litter. He had too much brain. You could see him trying to think, to understand what was beyond any dog to understand. Life must have been a puzzle for him. He was the receptacle of all my misery and agitations. I believe I would have gone mad if it were not for him. He absorbed my madness, to his cost.

I used to sink into his body, and hide my tears in his ribs. And constantly, constantly, since he slept with me, and lay all day in my room, he was bound, being him, to feel what I felt, to feel what I thought, my emotions forced upon him.

He comforted me physically, while I inadvertently communicated, on the invisible wavelength that enables some animals to sense and share human stress, or calm, everything I should have concealed from him.

He was scared, as a puppy, by a yellow labrador retriever.

The army ranges on Salisbury plain are open to the public for the weekend, at Easter. Open and exposed, with a prehistoric air. Not barren, but not exactly bloom-

81

ing either. The village of Imber, whose inhabitants patriotically evacuated it, secure in the promise they could have it back after the war, has long been blown to pieces, only the church is intact, like a solitary virgin, and rectangular edifices, mockingly built on the sites of cottage gardens, present their flat faces and hollow eyes to the modern missile.

It must be odd, to be dead, and buried in the graveyard, still hallowed, cherished, and preserved, for ever England, with simulated war being waged above your head. An officer recently killed himself after a successful exercise. Nobody knew why. He stretched his body in some tattered bushes, under the song of the larks, and was not quickly found.

The billy goat is tethered to a hawthorn tree, on the edge of the plain above Warminster. I can hear the dog barking. Billy is furious, and unafraid. As soon as I appear on the scene, the dog seizes the goat by its scruff, and their combined strength breaks the goat's chain, whereupon, glued together as if in the throes of a weird copulation, they career off across a ploughed field, scum and lather and flecks of blood spraying out into the wind, from between the dog's jaws, into the path of the mistress, whose heart sinks deeper than her feet.

Billies are very tough, he was fine when I released him, and baity. I beat the dog. I located the owner, who took it well. An ill omen, though, in the land of the UFO, and desolation.

A rescued brown pony, which had been broken and ridden at two, was bought on an impulse, not mine, at a sale in the winter; and by the summer, was led up the ramp of the knacker's box, having revealed in addition to his parrot mouth sweet-itch and slipped stifles, smelling the stale blood, to be shot on the spot, and driven off with a trail of hot red stuff gushing noisily over the tailboard, leaving seemingly indelible dye on our gravel. His hind legs, sometimes one, sometimes both, would slip out of joint, without warning, and there he would be, dragging them behind him, semi-paralysed for several minutes: a tragic sight, and little you could do to help.

It began with my hens. If he was with my mother, he would stand with them pecking round his legs, as good as gold. But because they were my hens, I fed them, vanished to collect eggs, fussed over them, he developed an urge to catch them, and tease them, and punishment made it worse, compounding the jealousy, naughtiness, and instincts he couldn't control in himself, however he tried, and he did, visibly, try.

Beatings, dead hens hung on his neck, nothing was the least use. He continued to accompany Ma into the field, without difficulty, but if I was there it was hopeless. A check cord would never have deceived him, had it been as thin as cotton; but he would have broken it, or pulled me over; on a lunging rein he would have walked meekly beside me, with all of it coiled in my hand. One day, when he was with me on the other side of the hedge, he caught a glimpse of the hens and was off, deaf to calling, to bully them. A dead hen painted with mustard. Himself tied up, and bored, amongst them. It made it into a *thing* . . . too much anxiety, too much tension. I was guilty and upset if the hens suffered. He was no ordinary chicken killer; in fact, he didn't kill, simply mauled a single bird to the extent that she nodded off and died. He wasn't interested in other people's poultry, though in due course pigs drove him wild and he would quiver and shake at the faintest scent of them. True to his distant ancestry.

83

I am standing in a stable yard, talking to a girl about a pony I want her to take on for schooling. Her pet calf, which roams free, and my dog have been side by side, much the same height, the calf a paler fawn, and nose to nose, apparently having a conversation of sorts; the girl and I are smiling at the two of them. Seconds before I am ready to go, and call him to the car, the calf moves quickly out of the shadows of the yard, and is silhouetted against green grass and the red and white of the jump poles and the brown of the dung heap, transforming itself somehow from calf, from pet, from beast you behave yourself with, to flashing running prey. Interminably, we all ran round and round the dung heap, faster and faster, chasing our tails, in a nightmare. Then he leaped, and throwing his weight against the calf's shoulder – as his dam, the sweetest, gentlest animal, had, playing, taught her son; as their ancestors had tackled the boar – and the calf was down. He lay on it, worrying at its throat. I put my hand inside his mouth – falling on him – and as he always was to do, he let go.

They had soft mouths. They could both carry an egg without breaking it, with the greatest of ease. Their mouths were so wet and sloppy a captured mouse could creep out unnoticed.

I beat him. I had to, for the sake of appearances. I thought I had to, but it must, in retrospect, have made it worse. This was before the goat.

Their favourite game was bringing down the boar, launching themselves at each other at top speed, with a strange light in their eyes. It's not something you can prevent them from doing, unless you exercise them on a lead from a bicycle, and anyway, it's lovely to watch. But she never made use of it, except in play with him, and with her other puppies if they stayed with us until they were old enough to be initiated. I think there was one that did.

He was sweet with her puppies.

A yellow labrador frightened him at an impressionable age. It must have seemed ferocious. I should have avoided the lane where that yellow labrador lived. It was my first mistake.

A big dog must be *perfect* in temperament and manners, with other dogs, because of his size, and power, and immense strength, and his height. I learnt, many months later, that I couldn't trust him with yellow labradors; though in the intervening months of his adolescence I could; it was as if he abruptly remembered; harked back. On his home ground, he became unpredictable; away from home he was all right. But yellow labradors were, in the place we had now moved to, a small town, rather ubiquitous.

He could tell a black labrador from a yellow, and, more surprisingly, a yellow from a red-coated. The blacks were immune, the red he stared at and dismissed. It was only labradors, and only the yellows, that did the unkind trick in his head.

He was not, as a rule, out of my control. I cannot explain: how something seemed to snap – in his mind. His eyes would take on an unfamiliar glint – not that of the game – and he would be, very swiftly and suddenly, beyond me, beyond recall; and once he was lost to me like that, I had to run; and I had to act.

An old, old, old, old labrador, and an owner who is – if I had but known it – extremely short-sighted. He has already turned on her dog, and shaken him brutally; he has turned on another one or two, and has made a reputation for himself – after all, he towers above lab-radors, it is terrible.

I am walking by the river, and the land in front of me is clear. In some way I don't really understand when I think about it, she comes into the lower field, behind me, without, because she is half blind, seeing me. He looks back. I look at him, and I look back. I take steps forward, trusting he'll follow if I whistle naturally. It is touch and go. He gallops towards her dog and after a ghastly pause attacks it. I am stumbling across the rutted turf. The woman is shrieking. I am racing.

I have to put my hand into his mouth – he could break the bones if he bit hard, but he won't. I don't recommend it as a method of separating fighting dogs – the labrador was past snarling. I feel my voice drumming into his brain, and the huge teeth and jaw drop.

I beat him though I want to hug him, hug him and cry.

The silly woman is so distressed, she proceeds to take her ancient one – dogs usually respect age, mine doesn't – on a trek of miles and miles; and when she reaches her cottage, she doesn't examine her dog for marks, because she is upset. In a matter of days, her dog has an abscess on its neck, where a tooth penetrated the skin, the skin having closed over the infection. Her dog is consequently very ill, and what with the shock nearly dies.

I can remember the running over the grass, and the distance it was; and the sensation of not getting any-where.

There was a wooded hillside, like a broad back, where I used to walk, to struggle with myself, while the dogs could safely plunge through empty briars and ferns.

I wanted to kill him myself. I understood how people gave their favourite spaniels or pointers or setters a choice dinner, and then took them out to a lonely glade, with a gun, returning to the house with an absence transparent at their heels. I dreaded the business of it, the civilised way. I wanted to kill him painlessly, inconspicuously, privately; for it to be a thing between just him and me; in love, in peace, in quiet. In grief.

I couldn't devise for him a regime of total and absolute restraint: of life cooped up indoors, and outings confined to the lead. It would have been unkind. He had not been brought up to it.

He was a brave dog.

From the subterranean quarries, the air rose through holes in the rocks, and being of a warmer temperature, stirred the plants and fronds that had grown over them. In the frosty weather, they breathed steam; and in all seasons were a source of mystery, and subtle danger.

Those beatings, ripping off my belt, or searching for a stick: if I could have shaken him half to death it might have been better; but I couldn't shake an animal of his size: those stupid beatings – he was not a dog to be beaten.

And I with my feeble blows had exerted an emotional pressure on him – which was worse than the heftiest striking, and confused him – he never attempted to avoid.

I was expected to act – as always one is forced to act – and, this time, drastically. I had to do, I supposed, what was expected of me. They were waiting for me. To offer them their retribution. To dish it up on a plate. No doubt.

But it wasn't like that at all. I am not so considerate. I would not have destroyed my dog even if the sentiments of the whole world were aroused against me.

I couldn't have a dog which savaged other, smaller dogs. Besides the domestic beasts and fowls. It was wrong. He had gone too far. *This was a matter entirely between him and me.*

I wished we could have run away. For us, there couldn't be a fresh beginning. I was trapped by my situation. I had to stay where I was. I had to. And to make my sacrifice.

I consulted our vet, a man I respected, the best small animals man I've known. Small animals. Into this small animal it was decided he should inject a substance which would have the effect of temporarily castrating him. If his aggression was of that nature, and if castration would cure it, I would have him castrated. It was doubtful that it was. And not the slightest bit of difference did it make. As the yellow labradors hove into view, he transformed himself into a vision of apoplectic, demented rage – he was a war dance on the end of his lead – and caused people to whiten and shrink with fear. You might suppose he would have pulled my mother, who was neither strong nor well, over, on the steep, icy slopes and flights of steps; but no, he took care of her, behaved with circumspection, and was his usual gentle self. I used to dread the rare day I would have to go away and leave her to cope with morning and evening walks: nothing untoward ever happened. At this point, I have also to refute the suggestion that I could have found him a good home. I could not. He had chosen me. Tiny puppies that choose never waver in their love and if you sell them in ignorance of it they pine and fret until you exchange them for a litter brother – my mother once had a dog that did precisely that.

Never would he have accepted another home, another

someone in my stead. There was no question about it. It wouldn't have been fair.

A week ... ten days ... passed: and, his ardours undiminished, I took him to be put down.

I had to blanket my mind, to hide all my conscious and unconscious thoughts from him: he must sense nothing, suspect nothing. I had at last learned with horses how to let a barrier fall, but, merely, not to betray nervousness. It would be infinitely more tricky to deceive him, he was more complicated than a horse. If I possibly could, I had to. I knew what to do, psychologically, and how to do it. I strained everything I had in me, to do that much for him. I think I succeeded, for the first and only time in his life.

I had to sign a form for him.

He sat down on the surgery floor and held out his foreleg while the barbiturate was injected into the vein. The expression on his face changed from a sheepish trust to enormous surprise, and then he wobbled, and sank; and the man helped him to lie flat out, and reached for a stethoscope.

He was unconscious but not dead.

He was rather difficult to kill, the dose required not being easy to calculate. Our vet lifted gravely his long tongue and sped a second shot, through the vein beneath it, to his heart. It was all over.

I fetched the thick rug from the car, and between us we lugged his extraordinarily heavy body there. The vet had a chronically bad back, I knew, so it was a trifle inconsiderate. I couldn't leave him to be made into soap. Animals weigh more when they are dead. Like humans. They are dead weights.

The petrol attendant, halfway on my journey, remarked on how fast asleep he was. He moved. He

89

stretched after a few miles. Because I didn't return home. I drove forty miles in the opposite direction, and my mother must have wondered where on earth I'd gone.

At the place I had, without stopping to think, without anticipation, torn to, along roads familiar since my childhood, no one was at that moment in. I hunted for the iron key and unlocked the door. I made a telephone call. I walked in the woods.

I left my mother wondering.

I believed, mistakenly, she had been lacking in understanding, for she had been tougher than I could bear.

I believed my two aunts could and would understand. And they did. Together, we hacked and picked, and dug a hole – we dug for hours, all afternoon we dug – through heath and peat and the gravel below: we pulled him from the back of the car, into a wheelbarrow, and tipped, I tipped him. There was no alternative. It hurt me to have to shovel earth on his *head*. And there he still is. In the wild shrubs. I seem to remember, with his collar on. A cup of tea. And a steering wheel pitted with his neurotic teethmarks. Oh, oh, oh, *be as thou wast wont to be, see as thou wast wont to see.* It's seven o'clock of a winter morning, and all's well.

I wish the wind would drop; the east wind; it ravages me. I am raw.

I smile at duck from the ponds crossing the black, clouded sky.

The yellow light: stumbling backwards, out into the dark, the wet, the outside. Not in the warmth. It is a rich yellow, and orange as the sun, and in it people dwell. In every patch a papa, a mama, and their heart-shaped-faced children, a family circle, complete, into which I

90

intrude. The mama is sewing, or reading to the children, or the children are reciting their tables. The papa has his book on his knee, under the lamp. I am a moth.

They are all they need, they turn to each other. They breathe contentment. It is only a picture. But much yellow light, much warmth in the house; and it is always cold without. In the fireplace are pretty flames.

There is a story by Oscar Wilde called *The Happy Prince*. You know it. A long time ago, when I was a little girl, it must have entered my consciousness, and it has never departed. I have, because of it, a clear image of how it feels for a heart to break. A leaden clunk. A split, a crack inside the body.

Families break my heart.

It may be maudlin but it is so. And on the occasions I hear that leaden clunk I am as if bereft of speech, something rises in my gorge, and I am filled with emotion. I am utterly undone.

Culpa mea.

No doubt a devil I should thrust behind me. It is involuntary. It happens before I can help it. It is too quick for me, too quick.

I think: it would be dreadful if it was known I was mentally slipping backwards out of houses consumed in longing to be enfolded.

I am injured by the fleeting expressions on other people's faces. The wistful, red-dressed spinster, who was lonely on a tourist trip in a bus. But for the grace of God went I there.

Lord, lettest thou thy servant; Lord, lettest thy servant; thou thy servant; me thy servant; thou; depart in peace, in peace, in peace, in peace; depart in peace; according to thy . . . word. Nunc dimittis; now dismiss us; me; let us

91

leave; me; now . . . Lord, lettest now thy now lettest thou thy now Lord lettest thou thy servant depart; in peace; according to. I mourn the children I might have had, according to the ages they might have been; no longer a desire for babies; a regret, an emptiness for growing children; and perhaps, some day, I shall arrive at grand-children.

Our father; which art in heaven; hallowed be; thy name; thy kingdom come; thy will be done; on earth; as it is in heaven; forgive us; this day; give us this day our daily bread; and forgive us our trespasses; as we forgive them that; trespass against us; and lead us not; into temptation and deliver us; from evil. Amen. For thine is the power; for thine is the kingdom the power and the glory for ever and ever and ever amen.

Stuttering, incantatory, a strange, unidentifiable distress: my hand trembles for no reason at all, at the words it is required to write, my lips stumble over speech, my foot trips, my memory . . .

I believe in God the Father, God; I believe in one God . . . but I don't, and am I not scrupulous, never to repeat any creed when I find myself in church. The peace which passeth all understanding; that peace; which has fascinated and tantalised me; be with you all; now and for evermore; evermore be with you; and for ever.

The closing of ranks: families, when ill. I feel a kind of desolate envy, which is worse than being alone – with coughs and colds and flu and sore throats.

I am good at looking after people in bed; my mother was too. It is simply a knack: suitable food, drinks, the right things to do to make someone comfy. I can't pretend it's nice to be ill on my own. The double-meaning comfort missed.

Lighten our darkness we beseech thee O Lord; lighten our darkness; we beseech thee; O Lord, that in . . . our darkness; lighten we beseech thee darkness we beseech thee lighten our darkness . . . darkness. Shadows of the night. Put to flight. Fleeing shadows this long night which is not a night but a life. Or part of a life.

Not coughs and colds and flu and sore throats. Properly ill.

To live one's life, a frightening disappointment, *right,* a superhuman task. The child said: You choose to be lonely. Do I? Do I? Did he mean lonely, or alone. Does it matter what he said? Does it matter what he meant, in the face of what he said?

In the beginning; as it was in the beginning; my soul, my soul, doth magnify; the Lord; and my spirit hath rejoiced in Go . . od my Saviour. O sing unto the Lord a new song for he hath done marvellous things.

Always on the fringe of other people's lives; left hovering; watching them to bed; to love each other; to fuck; loving their children by their permission, their generosity; and it is a very particular, peculiar generosity; loving them with my hands off: never, never, expecting, anything, and sometimes being, therefore, surprised.

. . . defend us from all perils and dangers of . . .

Abide with me; soft falls the; fast falls the; while shepherds watched their, washed their socks by night; there is a green field; far away; we plough the fields and scat . . ter; the good seed on the land.

God be in my head, and in my understanding. God be in my head. And in my. Understanding. Ole King Cole was a merry old soul. Five and twenty black birds. Baked in a pie. Cavaliers and roundheads.

On the ground. Not land. Ground. On the ground.

93

I lay down in a wood in Devon, once; and I thought, this is where I could die; in the open air; flat on my back; with a pattern, a mesmerising pattern of branches and blue sky to look up at; but like an animal, crawling to a separate place, away from its lair.

Hard ground, soft death. A coward's yellow death. A surrender. To an easeful, unmelancholy death.

I have fallen often upon such places. At least two or three a twelvemonth, during the death-wish years, and after. I have not forgotten the idea, of dying, doing myself in; but it is in the past. That doesn't prevent me from being alert to the possibility. It is a fundamental part of me. I am aware of dying and death more than I am of birth and being born. I cannot, obviously, recall being born, though I witness the births of puppies, foals, calves, kittens, naked mice, and might thus be reminded. In the deaths of horses, sheep, and, for heaven's sake, humans; of dogs, and rats, and shrews – their corpses damp and flattened in the fields; of nestlings, with stumpy sodden feathers, tumbled or pitched out of a tree; I reflect my own. Dying my little deaths, in the rain.

A bright, cerulean sky, then. A figure, a man, spreadeagled under a ceiling of shifting green leaves, intricate beech leaves: one doesn't know if he is alive or dead. But if, to the contrary, he was lain beside a haystack, he would be alive, thou knowest. And there is his red turnip handkerchief and bottle of cider.

Robin Hood
Has gone to the wood
He'll come back again
If we are good

A stoat, transporting her young, each by the scruff, across fields, under gates, through hedges, by a stream:

in that suspended moment, as she ran back and forth, back and forth, more and more wearily, with her skull bobbing in the deep grass; making myself as still as the stunted trees and logs and hawthorn bushes, listening for the reproving squawks and chatter of birds, that told me she had regained her original house far to my right; waiting for her reappearance – following her race along the bank – and her disappearance, into those roots and brambles, whither she was moving; I could have died there.

I don't want death as a solution: to illness, poverty, the quality of life.

I don't want to die in my sleep: at least this experience, of all common to man, need not be denied me? I'm curious. I should like to be aware and conscious. It has seemed to me to be the mystery of mysteries. *How can I imagine what I do not know.* But I have become a little acquainted lately.

I hope there will be an infinitesimal pause between the ceasing of the functions of the body and the brain's total eclipse.

I have been very close to killing myself; twice. Both times before a Christmas, within days of it.

I blame the intensity of the Christmases of my child-hood; and later Christmases. The terrible excitement, the minding lest anything should occur to spoil it. That heightened emotional . . . atmosphere.

It would have been unthinkable to have allowed a stranger in, and disliked relations were beyond the pale. A jolly woman friend of my mother's was not forgiven by me for fiddling with the Christmas decorations. I cried under my bed. I saw Christmas in an aura of sacred and private ritual. It was wrong, though glorious. And the child grown up was doomed to a lifetime of Christmas agony. There is no trauma attached to birthdays: from my tenth, I had them at school.

In the days when I brooded and dwelt upon death, I considered – running it through my mind – the programme; the steps I should take; the arrangements. Should I not add a codicil to my will? Otherwise it might not be quite as I now wished it. I'd scribble a few letters, of course. But how appalling for their recipients. I'd scrumple them up again. How bothersome it would be – to whom? – to abandon my affairs in disorder.

The plan became very elaborate, extending over months – very tragic and nerve-racking. I'd sell my possessions, my books, the most beloved. And silver. The clock. The trouble is I love and I hate my things. Possessions, I sometimes feel, corrupt. The aesthetic simplicity of that aspect of monastic life. It's difficult for me to understand that possession is unrelated to reality: the owning of a horse compels one to be concerned and to mind about it for its livelong life; and I cannot polish my furniture for fear of awakening the juices of possession. By reality I imply rational. It is an instinct, possession – not a need.

It's not irrational to long to walk out, with a few books, on all of it: to leave bed, board, the tables and surfaces of reading and writing and eating, the curtains and the blankets dated 1912, the financial apparatus of rent and rates and electricity supply; to duck out; nothing irrational in that.

I should, naturally, travel: around the world.

I used fondly to imagine and select my own funeral. A Christian burial, to my surprise. It was only nostalgia. I remember the chemical uplift of church. Of the singing

96

and the praising and the lovely, sentimental prayers. I was christened. I do not believe in God. I do not believe in the deity of Christ. It may be that I know the comforter best. Burial is for the rich or the committed – an unnecessary luxury, a self-indulgence for unbelievers.

I would laugh because I had come near enough to grasp that when all's said and done – it *isn't* said and done – you are beyond the point of caring about your books, or seeing the world first, or spending the rest of your money, or altering your will, or making a list of your treasures, or finding a beautiful landscape to die in, or fussing over your body and the redemption of your soul: you are flopped full length on your sofa, in your own room, gazing your last on the blur of your bookshelves – for the innocent reason that it happens to be the way you are facing; you are gone beyond the physical life; you are too near the fathomless bottom, dear nothing and nothing dear; you are not murmuring, even, howl, howl, howl, howl, howl, though you may be conscious of what is dead and what is alive. You may just write a letter to someone, sounding cheerful. No, that's not true. Nothingness. And numbness. And blank, without either desolation or will.

I was much fortified at school by the thought of my mother's emotion should some accident befall me. I felt gratified by the grief I was sure she would suffer, and harbour for some while to come. I liked to think of this metaphysical future for myself; in the same fashion I spent many hours after lights-out, aching to pee, aware that I'd have an order mark from still-prowling Matron if she caught me – and she would catch me – on the journey to the lavatory, wondering where my *mind* was: in my heart? in my head? in the middle of my body? It's a trifle

Whenne mine eynen misteth
And mine eren sisseth
And my nose coldeth
And my tunge foldeth
And my rude slaketh
And mine lippes blaketh
And my mouth grenneth
And my spotel renneth
And myn her riseth
And myne herte griseth
And mine handen bivieth
And mine feet stivieth —
Al to late, al to late
Whenne the bere is at the gate!

Thenne I shal flit
From bedde to flore
From flore to here
From here to bere
From bere to pit
And the pit fordit
Thenne lith myn hous uppe myn nese:
Of al this world ne give ich a pese!

odd it should have mattered.

Someone has to clear up the mess, whether it is premeditated or it is not.

I don't much care what happens to me. I used to have a fear of being buried alive.

The infant budded leaves, I want to take a cluster and stuff them into the cavity of my chest. Spring is slow coming, arrested by a cold snap. The black crow creaks as it flies by.

It was lucky, perhaps, that at the time I didn't realise how bad it was. I must have had an inkling of how it is to be mad. I spilt my brains. There was much losing of thread, my memory would be irretrievable, and then throw up, like ping pong balls on top of a fountain's jet, items from the past out of the reach of normal recall. One day, I found in my mouth every quotation I had ever learnt; a wink at exams; and an interminable procession of lines from Shakespeare, Keats, Shelley, made me feel demented. I begged for respite. It was uncontrollable, a twitch, a spasm.

I could do nothing, though I functioned as usual. I worked, but did not work. I read, but could not imagine. I did sums, but could not concentrate. I couldn't let go.

I woke with tears; cold tears, hot tea. I wept.

The blue tit peers into my room, with daring, to see if she can nest with me. She can't.

The fledgelings will drop like stones before flapping their already open wings, and flying.

It came to an end, between night and morning, in an unexpected paradise; of limitless well-being, and total happiness.

THE SEARCH FOR GOODBYE

If I had a daughter I should call her Jessie.

She would be a town child, whereas I was a country child.

I had my own garden, with marigolds, and shells, fossils, and stones; tiny lawns, and paths to stroll my fingers on; a special bed for my seeds.

I had an enormous garden – what would my daughter do?

Jessie would have nowhere to hide; no tree in which to build her house, or hang a hammock; no herbaceous border, no Michaelmas daisies; no barn, no loft, no orchard, no ditch, no hedge; no secret world, outside.

No pond to paddle in, with a ginger cat snug in his mint on the rim. No leeches to cling to her legs. No tics in the long grass, to be burnt off with lighted cigarettes. No fleas. And mosquitoes and midges would be holiday things. Grasshoppers cupped in her palms would give her the willies. She wouldn't find newts in the water trough.

I found newts in the water trough, in Farmer Cox's hundred acre, and I've never seen newts in a water trough since.

Jessie wouldn't know the smell of vegetables growing, or trust the innards of her life to unlocked doors.

No room to pitch her tent, no camp fire. No slackening of her guy ropes in the rain, no splicing, no practising of knots. She would wrinkle her nose at tarred twine – I used to press it beneath my nostrils: she wouldn't be that kind of person at all – and I think it's plastic nowadays.

She wouldn't listen for the strange, rasping cry of the dog fox when she's counting sheep.

Not for her the guilty thrill of hound music, and shivers down the spine. And if I were to be so stupid as to take her to a meet; if we then followed, on foot, or in the car, for an hour or two; she would send me to Coventry for a week.

Jessie would eat nothing but sausages and I shouldn't have the gumption – or the heart – to tell her what sausages are made of.

She would have to be accompanied everywhere. Otherwise it wouldn't be safe.

I had to be in by twilight. I sometimes drifted far afield.

But she would be at home on buses.

She would reckon that a Forestry Commission plantation is a nice wood to walk in. I'm afraid she might even whistle dogs in front of the friends who owned them.

She would be impractical, and hopeless with her hands. She wouldn't be able to split logs with an axe, chop kindling. She wouldn't have wanted to master a hook, or a scythe. I doubt if I would have allowed her to use a scythe until she was older. A fiendishly dangerous instrument.

She wouldn't have a clue about apples, how to pick them, how to store them: or pears.

Her childhood wouldn't be trodden on a stone floor; she wouldn't have stepped into a larder and felt its icy, still mystery; and she could never remember sharpening a knife and testing her courage by gutting a rabbit.

I must be permitted to see those years as idyllic.

104

The hymns, the psalms, the sounds and the tedium of Christianity: they would be as lost to her. I should be sad, but helpless. I can't show her Parson Griffith — he was Welsh — clumping up the aisle with his gumboots on under his cassock. I can't make her sit in a shiny pew listening to his red, inflammatory sermons, of which she might not understand a word. I can't take her to tea at the higgledy-piggledy rectory and protect her from his pinches. She'll never watch men and boys in their shirt sleeves ringing. She'll never have a turn at pumping the organ. She won't sing carols on Christmas Eve under a lantern, stamping and blowing, to the squeak of his fiddle: because his breed are dead.

She won't teach herself to swim in a river full of mud and weeds where a man drowned. Below the waterfall.

She won't wake and find the lanes are made impassable: by snow.

In London, there would be a grubby slush.

Oh, a great deal, did I, as a child, ponder the future of my children. Oh dearie me. Because there was always the thought that I couldn't bear to bring them up in a city.

And for the rest of my life, the city is a place where I retract my antennae. In the city I am oblivious of what, it has lately dawned on me, stimulates the townsfolk. In fact, I had it pointed out to me, and it was a revelation of stunning degree. The lights in the streets and the scent of exhaust are, apparently, attractive; and the noise to which I close my ears is reassuring while the quiet which I do not hear in the country is, I gather, disturbing.

I remember thinking: my children must grow up with animals, learn to ride, have dogs and cats and poultry, or they will be seriously deprived. The grown-up me would reject that as nonsense. Or would I? I am uneasy.

105

Of course we should have a cat, and not pity ourselves that we desire some kittens from the cat, before she is spayed, as an education, an experience, an event. Is that all? A few kittens and a guinea pig at school? Is a stream of matings and whelpings and hatchings necessary. The child expected children like herself. The grown-up wouldn't want it.

But there would be nothing with which to teach Jessie her duty towards animals; to put practical common sense before sentiment and emotion; to attend their deaths as well as their births, never to leave them until they are dead, never to abandon them to the vet, and to disregard one's own feelings; to feed them before oneself, and not late; to break ice on their water; to take notice of suffering always, never to leave rabbits shaking and blundering with pus – suppurating from their eyes – and swollen lids, if myxomatosis should return, never to pass by broken birds without knocking them on the head; to rescue large and small from snares, to pocket the snare wires; to provide for fattened beasts, if she must fatten beasts, the most civilised end available; and to ask the knacker, if the knacker it has to be, to shoot ponies at home.

Of all animals horses have the nicest lips, sensitive and dry, quivery and whiskery. I should so love to ride again.

I had to test my courage, rather more than with a dead baby rabbit, with riding, though I had a better head for heights, and might have proved myself in a more adequate manner in other directions.

As a very small child I sat well and was complimented; there was a gap when my old pony went lame – she was aged – and became not up to much thereafter. At ten and eleven I started riding with passion and I looked reasonably smart; but by my teens, embarrassing photographs reveal how dreadfully I now slouched; another chunk of years and, when I didn't care a hoot, a rare photograph or two, and I seem okay.

I wish I had sat better, though I think I had quite good hands. I didn't straighten my shoulders mentally until I was nearly grown up, and the physical followed.

Jessie will never know the pleasures and disciplines of riding every day, day after day, to exercise the horses. The secret satisfaction of jumping into private land, and cantering along the dark rides of large, defensive estates, trotting briskly across the front of the house, with a quick rattle round their rhododendrons, and out through the lodge gates: the excitement was to imagine someone minded, and I can't believe they did, or they would have said. I saw no one, neither keeper nor occupant.

I was keen, I lacked nerve.

I adored little thoroughbreds. I ought to have had a sweet, gentle creature unfortunately named Lucky: he broke down before I was due to try him – I rode him subsequently on another occasion and I know we should have suited – and in his stead we bought for me an equally sweet, neat-footed Irish mare: clipped out and kept in she would have been fine; as a grass-fed and presently winter-coated lazy dear, with two feeds of oats, and hay – and caked in mud – she was hard work. I would stare through her ears and try to miss the thickness of her poll, and the coarseness of her mane. She was marvellous out hunting: even if I was not.

Once I rode a dream. A hideous ewe-necked chestnut. Actually we were looking at a cob, intended for my mother, an iron grey of some malevolence called Granite. The man whose horses they were put me up on the chestnut, which must have been schooled for advanced dressage. I was, at a touch, able to perform the movements of my wildest and most futile ambition. It was almost unbelievable. He was a funny animal. I was ecstatic. That Granite meanwhile did his trick; a leap, without warning, into the air, like a rotten kind of capriole, though not from a standstill; calculated to dislodge a passenger and dump it on the ground. There was a chance of sticking on him, but he was not all that one desired for a lady.

I used to ride for hours, and miles, alone. A girl on a pony was relatively well armed against lechers, my mother thought. I had instructions not to let myself be pulled or tugged; to wield my stick or crop judiciously, and to clap my heels in, cantering away with aplomb.

I cherished my solitude.

Jessie wouldn't have been shy of boys her own age. Jessie wouldn't have been sent to a boarding school where the male sex was represented by the parson, the gardener, the art master, and, in the distance, choirboys. A nubile chum of mine carried on a spry correspondence with a choirboy.

Jessie wouldn't be emotionally castrated, tongue-tied, and utterly weary, from the years and years of fighting petty rules and regulations.

Three times in my life I have been burnt out; and the first time was at the end of school.

I was a nuisance. It seemed to me that protest mattered; that rebellion was not only romantic and just, to be pursued with dedication, but that it was an essential part of me, of my personality. I would begin and not have the wit to apply the brakes. Instinctively. I had much more fire in me in those days.

As a result, perhaps, of people being nasty to me at school, I was unpleasant at home, where I was always encouraged to talk and to take on visiting adults. The girl of fourteen could cause tempers to be lost or tears to be shed, often in humiliating circumstances. I could be as sarcastic as the spinsters I was exposed to in the term-time. I am not ashamed of the person I was then – who is another, and separate from me. I obviously admire her. I admire the spirit, the gumption she had, and I despise the cowed creature she became. And I hope that the mistress who scrawled in red ink, when I was ten, *dogs are not red* on my composition lived to regret it.

I had to have special permission to borrow books from the senior library: the precociousness, such as it was, was frowned on.

I was forced to change my handwriting, from the semi-copperplate my mother had taught me, to something simple, non-idiosyncratic. The idea was that we should all write similarly, and be easy to read.

I wasn't allowed to use a fountain pen, in the lower forms. In the second, third, and lower fourth forms, you dipped.

I was prevented from learning Greek, with the parson, because my reasons for wanting to were suspect.

Jessie wouldn't have had absurd tilts at authority.

I daresay she wouldn't have muttered lines of Keats and Shelley, like hair clutched by the handful, reeling in her senses, drunkenly: destined to spend a day twenty years later regorging every word she'd ever committed to memory, of Shakespeare, and the poets, English, Latin, and French, in an almighty effort to recall something much closer, which she has forgotten, it seems, for good. Finding her lips moving with this store-house.

109

There is a dialect word in my county, Dorset: I disre-member, for I can't, or I don't, remember. It's rare today to see people talking to themselves in the street. It used to be common. They don't whistle any more, either. I knew someone who whispered to herself in bed, and when dressing, undressing, unfastening her stays. I knew her terribly well.

I like to think, as my mother did, I could have broken the spell of slightly damaged, warped childhoods: absorbed and loving as she was in bringing up her chil-dren, my ma had had a bad mother, an unkind, unsatis-factory mother, a sad, sad figure, who raged and ranted and roared, rather.

I wanted a daughter, which is odd, seeing I have a softness for boys. I have wanted – God forgive me – to perpetuate myself. There is something of my mother in me. She was a better person than I am. It was many years before I realised that she was not as intelligent, not as wise, and more vulnerable, than I had assumed. She dominated me when I was grown up. She had a strong personality; and so, apparently, have I: hence, much clash and drumming of evocative memories, which were our ammunition, our battle cries. I argued that she had, for instance, chosen the wrong school for me. She had been impressed by the number of handbasins. And the rows of lavatories – how was she to have known we weren't allowed to use them? It wasn't really her fault: she had never been to school herself; and I should have been miserable anywhere.

Jessie wouldn't rip up precious things and desperately mourn them: as if to prove – they don't matter to me, or they matter too much to exist; as if willing to prick herself – if anyone is to hurt me, no one can hurt me more than I hurt myself.

In a tin trunk, my mother had stories and poems written by my brothers when they were little, together with my father's letters, family documents, wills, obituary notices, and birth certificates. I kept my own stories, and manuscripts – the prolific and serious beginnings *for books*. It occurred to me that she asked for theirs and hadn't asked for mine. Distraught, in tears, I burnt them. I have minded ever since. But my mother was horrified. I had only to mention I expected her to keep them – I didn't expect her to, and would have resented the suggestion – and into the tin trunk they would safely have gone. I had destroyed what amounted to the fruits of my childish labours and imagination without a word, *which was typical of me*.

I am worried that Jessie won't read. It would be my greatest dread – to accustom myself to a television child. A nonreader. I haven't a doubt that times are different. I like television. As television. But not in place of books.

Her life would have wider food for thought, spread thinner.

If I were a child today, though, I might well be spending my money on *Action Man*, instead of hoarding every penny, every postal order, every tip and token, to buy books.

I am still half buried in that world. I cannot imagine how it would have been without books, and the act of owning them. If to be grown up is to be stolidly indifferent to reality and not to hanker after transforming it – I don't think for a minute it is – I have not grown up. I want, when I look, to see something which isn't there, or not to see something which is there. I have been led on journeys to bits of Britain I held once in my grip, my

111

thrall, from Fort William to Coate. I have been often disappointed; either by the author, or by progress.

Jessie would find boring the characters on which I based my idea of myself: endlessly did I rehearse for my life in the wild, with leaves and billy cans, hammock and tent, bracken bed and groundsheet, a stone or brick hearth, invisible hedgehogs cooked in mud, a hazel spit, a jack knife, and pemmican, knowing I could kill a rabbit if I had need to eat.

Jessie would have no sympathy for the myth of the greenwood; no dream of being an outlaw; no sense of trees' clothing and protecting her – she would feel the damp and the drips. A cosy, complete, limited life, with the bole of an old oak as a house; food and warmth, and the prettiest ceiling on earth: I suppose it is daft. It is also private.

The romantic, magical forest: to melt into its vastness, be a lost human, to be sheltered, to hide, saying, this is where I am secure – in bed with *Bambi, The Story of a Red Deer,* and *Wild Lone.* The stag: running with head and antlers thrown back, antlers lain on his shoulders, reveals to the initiated, by the width of his path through thick undergrowth, and the shape of his slot, his size, his age, the number of his points, that he is a stag, not a hind, and his speed, by the splay in the cleft of his hoof. To Robin Hood, a young male deer, the young male deer probably accompanying the stag, would have been a brocket. The red deer have calves, but the fallow deer, fawns. The white hart, a black fox, oh, how to track those impossible beasts.

Not for Jessie the heroic victims of chase and hunt, which linger unfashionably on in my mind.

I cannot see fresh snow with the criss-crossings of birds

and small animals, and icy branches, without being hauled back to another book by B.B. called *Brendon Chase*. It was not my own, it was borrowed. Children took to the woods in it. That should explain everything. It is the winter in the book I remember, though there must have been a summer.

Snow is the bringer of silence, and beauty, and danger to the fugitive. His world has changed during the course of the night. He is exposed. By his footprints.

The deer paw the white for the pale, yellowed green, baring the blades of grass and herb.

The clouds are like spilt milk.

Originally, clouds had names, which have been forgotten. Medieval man, no more than do we ordinary folk, talked not of cumulo-nimbus, stratus, cirrus, or even fair-weather cumulus.

Can any two skies ever be the same?

Timber, water, fire: sights and sounds, of flames and smoke, of drinking and lapping. A stream: the pain of staring for a long time at a tangible but ephemeral substance. The state of fluidity: the colours of the mind dissolving and reassembling. It is perception that alters, not perceiving. Perched on a flat bleached stone in the middle, I see the stone is swirling too.

It is the grown-up who is struck by images. The child accepts them without thinking. In an untrammelled gap between reading and dreaming I used to push whole chapters which, to my chagrin, I found later not to exist in print.

Arthur Ransome did not fail me. The lake country was exactly as I had imagined it. The configuration of rock, and fell, and water which seems to me unique. I can't recall why I headed, first, for Ullswater, and discovered

Coniston anon. I came from Windermere over the Kirkstone Pass. I was exhausted, and it was twilight of peculiar darkness. I was desperate, along the shore of Ullswater, for a place to stop and sleep at. I could see the sheen on the surface of the water; I could smell the air; no more. By luck, that evening, there was no one camping in a dormobile, no one sitting up, four or five to a saloon car, no one at all, at what has become my lay-by; gravelled and guarded by twin litter-bins, modern equivalent of griffins; and I faced my bonnet to the lake. The beam of the moon was to shine directly into the car. Suspended above the lumps of hills on the far side of the lake was the full and orange moon herself. The trees stood very still, and across their roots a slivery sand, a yellow bar of beach, a few yards deep, was framed. The water foamed at the edge, and, as my eyes adjusted to the sombre light, I could pick out stones sticking through the shallows. I spread my things on the sand, and hollowed it to fit me. I abandoned myself to the balm of the air, and the dew falling, and the climbing of the moon, the dream in silhouette; at half-past five, the sun rose like toast; I waded in and swam.

The raw material, then, at Coniston. The main road round the lake in the blur between fantasy and fact gave me Wild Cat Island and Holly Howe. The east shore road, Horseshoe Cove, and Beckfoot. I had to reckon Windermere for Rio. I slept at the lakeside at Coniston too, like a dog lifting his leg on old territory, where there is a tiny promontory, with tall pine trees; and the wooded slopes of the fell behind, up which I galumphed in wellington boots to dig my hole and shit.

I wanted to go to Torcello because of a trashy novel, *Illyrian Spring*, by Ann Bridge. Jessie won't understand

114

such obsessions. I wish they would suffer a drought. As soon as I rid myself of one, another pierces the memory dam, and flows in fine spate. Obsolete recollections take charge of me and send me miles out of my way.

But I never return to places where I have lived.

Jessie will not walk with me beside my river, or finger lovingly the walls of my houses. I am a child no longer. Three houses fuse into a single experience. Grown up, daughter-at-home houses.

A house isolated in the midst of flat land which had a straight white road across it and rectangular fields cut out of a marshy common at the time of the enclosures, and the cry of the curlews nesting, though their natural habitat has vanished.

A house in a valley.

The swallows gathering on the telegraph wire to chatter to me while I worked in the garden. I did a man's job during the day, for a man's wages, and amongst men, in that remote country part, before the era of women's rights, and it was not questioned. I did my hard, physical job from eight o'clock, with ten minutes for lunch and half an hour for dinner, until five or four-thirty in winter, five-thirty in the summer; I came in to tea, and then did something else hard and physical until ten. I conformed to the pattern of life around me: every man did the same.

I can hear the squawks and cackles of my hens, if I listen, though I am years away. I can smell the soap suds with which I took arms against blackfly and greenfly. I have the hose in my hand and am watering the clay, the rich clay, cracked in a heatwave. I can taste my cabbages and potatoes, spinach and kale, carrots, onions, and shallots. I remember the strawberries ripening inside jam

115

jars, the gooseberry and currant bushes, the rhubarb on a bed of manure forced up a tall terracotta chimney pot. I remember the healing, soothing properties of earth, and of new-laid eggs, and of the scent of the sweet peas. I remember happiness.

A house in a town.

The bulging river, the opaque canal, the shining railway, like honeysuckle and two bindweeds. Jessie's ears may be keen but she won't catch the slender, wistful piping of dog whistles on the wind, down the line of the elm hedge. She'll not see the green woodpecker; the kingfishers; the dragonflies; the old heron; the swans; the chestnuts breaking into open fists each spring; the red soil from the distant Cotswolds in the flood; the perfect, photographic reflections. In a copse near the shot tower and the derelict mill I found a rubbish shute. I gazed, from the foot of it, up at the rusting metal and the sodden paper sacks, the rags, the bottles, the broken glass, the jarringly ugly refuse: it was lit by the sun sifting through some larches, and bluebells were growing in it. And I thought, how beautiful.

I forget the dull days.

A house of illnesses and rats. I shod a pony. The blacksmith was over sixty and had lost his nerve. It was a slightly temperamental four-year-old's first shoeing. I had to have the hind shoes on. I was scared of pricking him, not of being kicked. A horsenail is bevelled at the point so that as it is driven through the hoof it bends. If I didn't make the appalling mistake of facing the bevel the wrong way – and that I simply had not to do – I might have sent the nails too high. The pony might have fussed, attempted to take his foot away, bang his leg down with but two nails in, twisting the shoe so the nails would be

116

half drawn, and the whole business started again. Seven nails – and each to be caught off in the hammer, each potential rippers of the hand, and then clinched. The blacksmith had put his front shoes on a couple of weeks before. I am proud of having shod him behind. I did it. And those shoes stayed on. A rough job, but comfortable – as proved.

I am proud of the seventeen – I have counted – horses and ponies which passed through our hands from my earliest childhood to that unexpected echo of it when I was grown up. I can turn them over in my mind like lovers.

If I had a daughter . . . I should call her Goodbye.

I am trapped in my London flat. Terrible, booming music rises as if from the bowels of my earth. I want to bid farewell to the piece of myself that is . . . has gone . . . missing. And I cannot.

I am neither of the town nor of the country now. I am forever torn between them. Longing, in the town, for something of the country. In the country, needing something it can't provide. A stranger here and estranged from there. I remember the reclusiveness into which I dropped. I should not be immune from it if I withdrew. I am not so unsophisticated I don't fear the country, where spinster-status is degrading, where married girls of nineteen are respectfully called Missus, and unmarried women by their Christian names until the grave: and where it is beholden that people should pester you about your man. The country can be quite cruel. But the pavements are stained with sick, are swimming in foul litter and dust. I am frightened of people behind me. I am tired of hearing other people eating their breakfasts with clanging spoons, their footfalls, their awful voices.

117

I am constantly panting to disentangle myself, for a moment, long moments, from the city, and no amount of tramping around the travesties of countryside it boasts will cure me. As that other, ballad Robin Hood, pining for the forest, for the greenwood tree, unable to bear living at the court of the King, seeks an excuse to absent himself for a short while. But he never returns.

Time slips – truly.

I find myself an hour later though I feel a mere second has elapsed. There is a nothingness in London time. Slipped time.

In London no life; no ditches; no hedgerows; no death. No worms, no bugs; no thorns, no wire. No cattle, no stock of any sort. No thrills and no excitement. It is undramatic.

In extremes of hope and sadness the wind will cease abruptly. The stars are switched on; or the sky is glowering, black. Sprig and leaf are emerald, bilious, rusty, and then slush. The agitated bellies of sailor-suited swallows circle to retrieve their direction. The slim thrush, digging a hole for grubs, dirties his beak.

I have discovered an amazing gift in myself, a boon. For the first three or four hours in rural solitude and peace, my senses expand so rapidly that I can smell separate varieties of grass and trees, bracken or gorse or heather, buttercup or vetch, I can scent cow or pig or horse, fox or badger, manure or silage, hay or straw, burning and steaming and decaying: depending on the season, on the lie of the land, and its nature. It makes me giddy.

But the country is a great deceiver. Because it is, of course, no longer there: the land of my imagination. I have been bending over a rose, sniffing and sniffing; and

118

the rose is blown. A lot of the country has become ghastly. Bungaloid, obliterated, crowded, and spoiled. It is . . . progress.

The journey to a morsel of peace is fraught with eye-sores. It is emotionally arduous; so arduous that I finally prefer to stay at home. *Until only to think is to have gone.* There is a limit to my ability, however, to project myself — outwards to the hills and brooks and woods and fields, not as a human being but an abstract bundle, bowling around like a pumpkin, weightless and invisible. I don't live in my mind, I live outside it. If I see some mown, unturned hay, I want to get into bed with it, pull it up to my chin like an eiderdown, pull it over my head, bury my face in it. I couldn't be more ridiculous.

I am too often anguished and disappointed at the end of a proper, bodily journey. It takes too long to obtain a minute of ecstasy. I have to go further, and further, to be alone. But one summer, I went far enough. To Scotland. Beyond my known northern boundary.

At first light, I came to Loch Earn. The sunshine began to strengthen and flow. I could warm myself, stretch myself, I could make coffee and eat a marmalade bun on the shore-wall. Not a soul . . . nothing stirring but a lone black-headed gull on a stone in the shallows. The loch was smooth, limpid, shimmering very slightly with reflections of the hills, which themselves were sharply divided into shadow and life. I was well slept. The place had a . . .

119

clean spirit. I jumped down, and balanced, in this spell-binding morning, like the gull, on a stone. Beneath the surface, the pebbles, and far away the clear water becoming uninterpretable. The water rippled as I dipped my hands; with my right hand I lifted the water into the air and let it drop; I lifted it and let it fall through my fingers; I gazed terribly hard at this beauty; and wished, at the third time, with every ounce of wishing energy. Bless, heal me, I must have said. The water did its best.

If I stood, or huddled quietly, beasts arrived; birds, with strange, striated plumage, appeared from nowhere out of bushes, juniper bushes, and sang; odd songs I hadn't heard before. Without a dog, I saw as I'd never seen before, and heard shy things. I am discountenanced without a dog to walk with, but it brought compensations. The small red squirrel sat in the tree, the small brown hawk perched on a neighbouring branch. I crouched in a hollow moulded by a sheep and smelly, the sandy soil bared under a grass overhang; with tiny fir-cones, needles, bone-dry dung; out of the wind, with my thermos and sandwiches, fortifying dates, and apple; and the burn's bed, to which precipitous fragments would, undislodged, fall, below. The bird and the animal were unaware of the human. The animal hadn't noticed the bird as it sank from the sky into the trees – alder, rowan, fir, oak. The hawk was motionless, watching. It thought to chivy the squirrel: awkwardly, as there was no real wing space; half flying, fluttering, hop hopping; and the burnished, red squirrel ran. It seemed to be a rather youthful squirrel. As it ran instinctively round to the rear of the tree trunks to disguise its departure, the hawk tilted after it. The female merlin, for so she was, I believe, looked intensely interested. The squirrel was unnerved: it tore towards me, clattering its claws down the bark of a spar. The hawk bounced, almost landing upon the squirrel's now paralysed, cocked head. The squirrel, obviously shocked out of its wits, somersaulted to the roots, and made off on all fours, in a manner reminiscent of a cringing spaniel. The hawk rose indolently, and settled by the fork of a fir branch; she sheathed her wings; I stared at her beak. Then she flew.

I followed, for an hour, sheep tracks; and when it was time to leave the burn, I left the scant shade too. I struck across a morass of burnt heather, on the lower flank of the mountain. The summit, from there, was hidden. I aimed for a greenish streak, one of the two water-courses visible from a distance. After the ashy field of pain I was keen to tackle the steepness. I met a large rock: leaning against it, I rested. A gurgling sounded through the crevices. In the squidge I couldn't make a puddle of even a mouthful. I dragged at the swarming flies with a switch. They treated me as if my eyes belonged to a horse or a cow. Already the perspective was different – I was higher than I had reckoned. Holding to tufts and sprigs, my belly damp, I hauled myself up, and up; scrabbling with hands and knees and toes. The sun was hard on my neck. The heat of the noonday was affecting my heart. It banged horribly. Above me: endless deceptions of skyline. I was exhausted. I was bursting with energy. I wanted to stop, and I was afraid I would give up. I wasn't fit, my legs trembled. The ling, irritant and dusty, penetrated my socks. I rested. I tried to take bearings. I trod warily across slanted, ankle-twisting, slippery rocks. I reached heather as tall as my thighs, through which I

121

walked . . . struggled . . . blind. I was at the base of a near-perpendicular, lemon-green sog, of twelve to fifteen feet. I thrust myself up it. I was soaking wet. I felt there was still a great height of mountain. I saw an outcrop I recognised, or fancied I did. But when I stood, dizzily, on my two feet, I saw, to my surprise, I was quite close to the top. I had to do no more than extend one leg after another, on the soft peat. A spring's rising had created a deep depression. The earth was cracked; but it was summer; and no water came. I squatted and made my own. I could stagger to the cairn on the summit, it was breathlessly simple, on the beaten track that switchbacks across the three mountains. I could look down, and see Loch Morlich, on the other side. The air was very fresh, and foreign, and cool. I was in heaven.

I stood brooding – into the waters of Loch an Eilein. A storm was announcing itself with waves, and dark thrashing, though the wind seemed to blow no stronger than usual, and the sun was bright. The water was full of portents, omens swam in it, malignity: how could it be so shrouded, while the sun shone on it; and why did those waves chop so angrily, flashing their mirrors. I stood brooding on the promontory by the monument, I contemplated the loch's agitation: I felt threatened. In my mind I flapped, with plaids and pipes and long black wigs; brogues with holes oozing; curly locks, eyeless sockets; lace handkerchiefs. And a real live storm was manifestly coming, from the crook of the loch, the bend in its arm, and from the shoulders of mountains. I tugged my hat over my brows.

I was a glacier. The gentle air in the glen blew furiously

and yanked at my hair: my scalp didn't hurt. The cele-
brated *roads* were attempting to intrigue my eye to the
curve of the land. All was sweetness and light. And
emptiness. I was alone. There was only a scarlet post-van,
lurching and roaring over the bumps into oblivion, soon
to return; on his forced march, the postman, no doubt.

Grateful for the taste of milk . . . nectar from cows that
drink magic Highland water: enchanted by the scent of
the meadow . . . vetch and buttercup and clover pollen
strewed before me: by the feathery grass and the crop-
ped grass . . . the blue ridges, the silver birch and rowan
trees allowed to grow and rot in the pastures . . . the
colouring, a delicate green: the shape of the trees stunted
and askew to an invisible gale: for the call of the grouse,
the rare and the common birds, for the little Green Loch;
for all wishes, for whitened wood, bleached bones, the
sour stink of the sheep, the melancholy decay . . .
gratitude too.

The hind sped past me, trailing silver drips from her
muzzle. I looked for the deer at sunset, when they were
impatient to drink after a hot day lying in the covert.

I remember thinking, how sad to uproot and destroy
such ancient hulks, with their clutching fingers, the
skeletons of the Caledonian Forest; ravaging them to
plant conifers in rows. I saw them twice. But the third
time I came to pass by them, they were gone, and I could
never find them again. The conifers were planted, they
were half-grown, adolescents. Absolutely nowhere was
there room for a tract of relics. Not in daylight. Not at
dusk. Not . . . today.

123

A light sandy fox, like a yellow labrador, basked in some ruined stone. I saw it across the standing hay – late hay: all the hay was slow to my southern mind. The rest of the field was sown with turnips. The fox spotted me. It stood, and stared at me, a long way off, its back sagged, relaxed. It presently sat on its haunches. I walked steadily on the track, turning my head every few moments to keep it in sight. I realised when I arrived at the junction of hay and turnip that the fox had lain, and was concealed from view by the height of the grass: it couldn't have gone, not over the slope, I should have seen it. I edged up the furrow between the crops, taking my time. At the end a wicket gate of wrought iron was wired into the fence. I saw the fox: at ease on the turf. I was downwind of him. It was comic, because he would hoist his muzzle, and scent, and scent nothing. It was as if without being able to smell me, he didn't see me, could not see me. I was motionless: now perhaps five yards distant. I had often walked up on a vixen and cubs – she had an earth in the bank at the top of our paddock – but with a pony; my hand in the pony's mane, my legs beside its legs, our scent mingling. I had never done it unaccompanied. I imitated a pillar for as long as I could. He must have seen me clearly. A mosquito struck; another hit my neck. I tried to steel myself to them. But I raised my hand involuntarily. In a split second, he had risen, unfussed, and vanished. He had a white tip to his brush.

I was lost in a drizzle. I tripped through a moon-landscape wood at nine o'clock in the evening: in and out, over and under, briars and thickets, over sinister moss-covered stones and boulders. I thought the silver birches, with their strange fungi, were sticking out their tongues

124

at me. I thought myself very mad, and stupid. I felt the curtain of mist was catching me. I found the burn, which was flush to the brim and deafeningly noisy, and followed it. I emerged abruptly from the copse on a seductive path I didn't recognise at all. I saw fields, a flat sleeper-bridge, a gate, a stile, more fields, a farm not far away. The washing hung heavily on the line, and rusty implements reclined in the bracken. I leant on the gate, looking for a clue as to where I might be. I turned . . . buildings, beehives, piles of timber, a blue rick-sheet . . . the blue rick-sheet, it was weirdly familiar. Truly, I quivered with shock. The gate, the water, the bridge: I had crossed them on the outward journey. But I had been so sure I was somewhere else; higher in the wood. I was safe, and the light was fading early.

The Glac Mhor stretched for two miles beneath the north-east side of the mountain. It was my favourite walk, lonely and neglected: in some cunning way, both sheltered and exposed. After the first burn, there were sheep; and fierce oystercatchers who felt it necessary to dive at the hats of passers-by to protect their nests. At the finish of the pasture-land, a fence was torn and tangled – its stakes moth-eaten and the wire in loops. I forced my legs like scissors through the heather. The path was one leg wide. A teeth-gritting exercise. But all of a sudden, like a heart's desire, I fell onto sweet, shorn grass, and cairns. The grass oblong was remarkable. It was bounded on the long parallel by tumbled, but still substantial, walling; otherwise it was open to the heather. It seemed that the heather obeyed strict and natural instructions. It thrived neatly at the edge; none grew within. This miracle was, I reckon, a Pictish cattle byre. The dung of

125

the Pictish beasts had caused a fertility which would preserve it eternally: the grass was grazed by animals that slept and ate and made more dung on it, through the centuries. It could never be corrupted. The Pictish graves were a trifle disturbed, and heather sprouted in them. I curled myself into one which was pure as snow. I spent half an hour in the sun, sweating into the Pictish grass, thinking how life would have been for them, aloft in the sky over Strathspey, with their custom of copulating in public. An ewe was bleeding from a horn. She was shaking and shaking her head. The blood ran quaintly over her eye. She bolted with her lamb, then halted and glared. The marking of these particular sheep was on the wither: they appeared to have severed necks. The heather thinned at last, and underfoot it was flinty. I had a track to walk on. Someone had ridden by. But not for a while, anyone: the rabbits scattered in front of me as I approached. The land was scarred, reclaimed from heather, burnt and beaten and white. The soil was silvery. The path dropped into the second burn. I could hear the sound of sheep penned for the clipping. I had lunch with my feet under the waterfall. Downstream the whole burn plummeted underground, though very undramatically: it just soaked away, the little torrent, into several holes. I continued my walk, and it was when I was coming back across the burn, pausing only to sip it, that I heard the mew of a cat. I was above the burn. I stood stock still. It was a wail, an unearthly shriek which reverberated in the desolation . . . it was eerie, and my hair crawled, shivers ran down my flesh. I laid my satchel on the heather and crept towards the racket, which I could locate as emanating from a rock pile with a single, sentinel tree, and scrubby bushes. I picked up a stick, and gripped it. No matter how cautiously I went, I would crack a twig soon, I realised: I waited, not moving. The wailing cut out like a shot. A tabby form, tail foremost, thick and black-hooped, swishing meanly, slid carefully to the foot of the tree, and melted — that deliberate cloaking of invisibility — into the rock: and with that extraordinary, slow-rapid, timeless movement which so fascinates me, three litter brothers or sisters were revealed. I wondered briefly if they were feral cats, but no, those were wild cat. To me, it was utterly, utterly thrilling. It was the nearest I have ever been to orgasm for no obviously sexual reason. I took up a position on the further bank, in a circle of vacant earths, to wait long and patiently for the wild cat to come out. But they did not.

I returned to the Highlands the following year, in late September. The birds of paradise, being summer visitors, had flown. The water of paradise tasted brackish after the drought. The weather was surly and blocked the sun. I was disconcerted by not once seeing the tops of the mountains. The superabundant animals of paradise — the deer, the foxes, the wild cat, the red squirrels, the rabbits, the brown hares on the moor — were as if they had never been. They were in their lairs and dens, or they kept to the hours of darkness.

DREAMING OF DEAD PEOPLE

I see her as she was six or seven years before she died.

It wasn't alarming until I began to dwell on it. And they come thick and frequent.

I am having a dream-life with someone I loved, and considered always, and shared images with, like cereals for breakfast: what could be more natural.

I hadn't dreamt, in my sleep, before she was dead, of anyone – as if alive – who was not alive. If I had, I'd forgotten. It disconcerted me.

I dream of two beings: my mother and my dog. They appear in new adventures, new chapters, in a kind of children's book half-life.

The memory of that afternoon, the afternoon I buried my dog, the other half of the day, the part which wasn't mine, but hers: discovering it. She had cried. She had gone upstairs to her room – you don't cry in the drawing room, whatever you do – and soaked a lot of hankies. I was dumbfounded.

I had believed she never would, never could. Never did. Cowards cried. Tears were weak. They were ridiculous. If I cried as a child, she invariably laughed, which I felt was nasty. I am still not certain if it stemmed from the desire to be bracing, or from embarrassment. I had never seen her shed a single tear. In the back of my mind was the idea she hadn't cried when my father was killed. I was much too often flooded with emotion myself: I quite admired her for it.

I suspect I have lice in my hair. I sit in a chair while she parts it and peers. I feel a strange, physical soothing all through my body, a purely instinctual response: we never touch; it is a novelty.

Comfort was a chilly, powerfully deep business. She pretended not to understand my outbursts: to submerge my feelings beneath a million stiff lips should have been my only aim; they weren't decent, otherwise.

I ache simply to pick up the telephone and talk to her. Not to moan – to chatter. I doubt if we were bored when together. I make efforts in my dreams to telephone her. I try and I try and I try, in epic agonies of lost numbers, not being able to persuade someone – who proves to be my sister-in-law – to call her to me, or to repeat to me the correct number; and of echoing kiosks and leaden directories; and a barrel which recently has had creosote in it.

It might have seemed undemonstrative – well, it was, my relationship with my mother. But there was something shared between us; something stiff and unyielding, fierce and loving. It was not merely by the accident of my father having died when I was three that she had such importance in my imagination.

I wonder how much *she* needed to be hugged. After my father was dead, and she was widowed, as old as I am. As young.

She wanted to see Venice before she died: it is not so much that she didn't, which bothers me; but that she knew before she died she never would.

Predictable, it is, I am, all is predictable.

If I stand on the balcony, at the prow, the corner, facing into the wind, and if the wind is strong, filled with rain, I can almost recollect being at sea. I have spent

132

seven months of my life at sea. Thank heaven. Ocean is another world. I may forget it; I shall not forget it is different. Twenty countries, I have been to. Ma had been to China, and I not east of Port Harcourt. I want to ride a camel, an elephant, see wild animals in the wild, India, and Thailand, and maybe Japan. She took Nannie to China.

Dear Lavinia, Is your cold better? I am glad you have started dancing on the grass. Does Nannie dance with you? I saw the King the other day. He was in the uniform of an Admiral of the Fleet, and I shook hands with him. Are the boys playing a lot of cricket?

Yes, I had a nanny. Nannie came back for me, having gone when the boys were big. I loved her. I loved her dearly. I used to puzzle: which would I choose, if I had to choose – Mummie or Nannie. *My comfortable old cap blew over the side last week. Most annoying. 'Bother', I say; though Nannie would probably say something stronger. Give Mummie a kiss for me please. I can't come home for a long time. How are Pearl and Fly and Jake? My bed time now: Goodnight. With love from Daddy.*

I didn't have to choose. Nannie couldn't be afforded, on a naval pension, when my father was found dead in the water.

In the nursery, we ate nursery meals – tapioca and brains; and she sewed and smocked while I played with my nineteen dolls. There was limed oak furniture, and a wicker chair painted blue and red round the edge, pictures by Cecil Aldin, and an oval mat on the floor which hung on for many years as a rug for the dogs to lie on in the car. Nannie had lines running from her cheeks to her mouth; I can feel the smile they made, and smell her skin. I can remember dreaming in my pram, fondling the fringe of the awning.

Our beds in the night nursery were close together, with blue cotton counterpanes, and paisley eiderdowns. Nannie slept through the air raid warnings. I would wake her; we would wrap ourselves up, hurry past the gate on the landing, and hide under the stairs, sucking a special kind of peppermint which was bomb-shaped and unspeakable.

Nannie refused point-blank to have evacuees. She wouldn't hear of it. Therefore my mother was a fire warden and out at night. Towards the end of the war, my mother scrubbed the kitchen floor on hands and knees because there was no one else to do it: in order to keep Nannie happy; and rather than let this essential, holy being out of my life so terribly soon.

In the garden, she lifted me up to finger the sundial. I popped the fuschia flowers on toddles round it; and in autumn, there were the huge copper leaves of the virginia creeper to shuffle through and gather in fistfuls. A hedgehog was trapped in the tennis court. I had two plain, stone rabbits I lugged by the ears.

Nannie left when I was four, and we moved house.

I thought at the time much about being buried alive: waking up in a coffin. I knew my father was in a grave in a place called Naples. It had to be possible for him to find his way out of it.

I dreamt repetitively: the dream of the empty rooms.

I dreamt I was a soul. A soul resembles a grey ball of cloud, which turns over and over instead of walking, like a pumpkin. All souls looked alike, but within each was an individual. As this soul I wafted in and out of sunsets, sat upon soft heaps in the sky, and danced the polka; but mostly the soul bowled along in a nightmare of empty

rooms; some large; some small; sometimes thirty or forty
– I didn't count them – identical; a baffling honeycomb;
and the poor soul despaired. But before I woke, I
arrived. The rooms delivered me. I was precipitated into
a vast, cavernous hall – heaven its ceiling – with steps,
hundreds and hundreds of steep steps. It was extremely
tiring, pushing through all the angels and the men – I
don't recall any women – who were dead. At the very top
was God. On the second step – the topmost step was
narrow and would accommodate only a single pair of feet
– and at God's right hand, stood Jesus; on God's left, or
right as I mount the interminable steps, and I do reach
the summit, at the other hand of God was my father,
holding his sword.

God was kind. He made complimentary remarks.

I woke, at this excellent moment: I never dreamt
beyond it.

I thought much about space: what it meant. I had
feelings of being whirled off into space and timelessness;
there was a physical pull; I lost contact with the sheets
and blankets; my brain would suddenly shoot upwards to
the ceiling, press against a corner as if wanting to escape.
I didn't want it to escape. I was terrified. I wanted to lie
flat in bed; in peace; ordinarily; and I could not.

Space was starless, sunless. Not dark, not light; moon-
less, and unmagical; unpleasant: it was the universe, the
concept of which I knew I couldn't understand. It wasn't
until I was older that I didn't mind its being there, not
understandable.

I thought about atom bombs.

I would hear a voice downstairs in the drawing room,
as I lay in bed. It was the Queen, the present Queen
Mother, come to explain *in person* to my mother that my

father had been on a secret mission; so secret that his family, unfortunately, had had to suffer and believe him dead; far from being dead, he was alive; and had been *very brave*. The pretty voice, floating up from the drawing room, would slowly impinge on my consciousness. I prolonged my delight, savouring it. I heard faint music, a naval band, and sailors marching in the village. I saw them in the lane, soldiers too. And the Household Cavalry. They were bringing my father home.

I could understand he was dead. *Luckily, Lavinia has some idea of heaven: she tells us Jesus is walking with Daddy in the fields.* I could not accept it. I hadn't forgotten him. *It was her Daddy's birthday today: she says Jesus has made him a birthday cake.* I remembered him. *She says, without mentioning Daddy, she is 'sad and lonely': the inevitable happened — Toby Sinclair asked her why her Daddy went to heaven, she answered instantly, 'Because he wanted to, of course . . . he couldn't stay in the sea without his ship'.* I remembered him deliberately, keeping the memories alive in my mind. The obsession dominated me until I was twelve. *The dreadful news came through that Lavinia hasn't a Daddy to come home to her any more.* I hadn't had my third birthday when, for the last time, he came home on leave. *I got Nannie to tell her: luckily, she has some idea of heaven from her set of Bible Stories.* I resurrected him, intensely, passionately. I dreamt, I wept, I slept beneath his crossed sword. Truly, I have been to Naples.

I had my hair cut like a boy's.

I knew Grandpa would die a couple of days before he did. I wanted him to be wearing his long woolly undergarments, ready for the cold trip to heaven. He had a dicky heart, but had been quite hale. I uttered twice — Ma was afraid I'd blurt something out in front of him — and

136

then he died, in the night.

I have tasted the future, occasionally, all my life.

Have I not the ability to pour boiling water over my hand, without feeling pain, or scalding the skin. I used my threescore and ten of howling at Lyme Regis, on the shingle beach: hot coffee was spilt on me, half bare, from a thermos.

I drove my dolls and me in a carriage, of upturned chairs and cushions, with a pair, in tandem.

I drew sailing dinghies, and boats with living quarters; I rigged them as well as I could, having no experience of boats, other than rowing with a picnic on the Stour at Wimborne; and I made them flags.

I spent hours naming my imaginary people, and their horses. I arrayed them in favourite colours: someone with red hair would have a green jersey; with black hair, blue or yellow. They wore polo-necked jerseys, buff breeches, and boots. They were full grown boy-men, capable of riding in a point-to-point race. Igor was of the species *Tom Thumb*. His chief duty was to crawl up inside me, between my legs, and supply me with children. He lived in the lavatory, the room where the lavatory was; and if I stayed away, he had to be a visitor to their lavatory as I was to their spare room. Our children remained — where they'd been born — in my bed, shoved into the tucks. Igor and I had a holiday, for several summers, with Nannie, who had married, in the Isle of Wight. I was five, six, seven. The riders beside trains easily outstripped him. They came to school with me. In fact, though I don't often travel by train . . . I am not absolutely *blind*.

There was a cupboard in my bedroom. It had in it: my clothes, the dressing-up box, a trunk or two; and could take two or three children with the door shut. In the

137

dark, or by torchlight, the son of the village baker and I poked coat-hangers at our groins and fingered each other; we may have reckoned we were doctors and nurses; without much ado we became fathers and mothers. He was my first great friend; when he was older, he was a pilot in the Royal Navy.

At boarding-school, we humped and thrust on eiderdowns in cupboards and hoped the mimicry was correct. I fumbled in bed with another girl; I was ten. A couple in the upper fifth were caught kissing – an atmosphere of horror and retribution ensued. Two of the mistresses were humping with impunity. Or so we thought. If we encountered lechery, in circumstances usually to do with music recitals, we were alarmed but not treacherous.

I broke my wrist carrying eight thick, white plates, from the kitchen hatch to the dining room. I also broke some of the plates, for which I was graciously not fined. I was sent home at the end of term with a sprain, and it had to be re-broken.

I was constitutionally unable to eat marrow, beetroot, and maggots in raspberries: to ask for a small helping was to receive double.

The rules bred, whilst I was incubating my capacity for misery, from a dozen to three dozen. The privileges decreased to nil.

The headmistress was saintly, a beautiful swineherd barged by porcine staff.

Missionaries, radiant, yellow, and shaking, Christians all, as we, brought lantern slides and films of lepers. At weekends we had cakes for tea.

At night in a high wind, the house swayed. I slept on the roof with my big toe tied to a chimney, and a rolled-up blanket deputising for me in bed. There were secret passages, and a ruined grotto with palms and tangle-ments; a broad terrace, with walls, and stone vases; azaleas in the garden; and a lake in the park.

In the park lurked Polish refugees to rape us, and strangle us if we screamed.

In the winter it was cold, the wind blew off the moor. Chills sat on the chest. As we wheezed, and struggled, and ached in our bones for some loving care, we learnt spine, singing, and what it was to be embittered women.

I hated school spirit, house spirit, team spirit, and any other surrender of my own spirit.

I lost my naval crown brooch 'helping' our headmistress with the chapel flowers. I searched and I searched among the rotting stalks and leaves. Ma lost her wedding ring because when she was ill and dying, her finger was thin. She searched and she searched. . . .

Too much longing for the end of term, dread sickness for the holidays ending. Brushing cheeks on the platform six times a year – oh, and at outings. You were so stiff, she once said. You don't realise what a forbidding child you were.

To take me out, she had to drive over a hundred miles there and back, on bad roads, with steep hills, in an ancient Singer.

I remember her bringing a litter of puppies and their mother, with meals of Farex and milk, and shredded raw meat.

I remember the pain of waiting; the emotion, bottled and corked; the sound of the car wheels on the peculiarly fine carriage sweep. The fear of time . . . passing. The exquisite relief and disorientation of the day. The picnic. The opening and the shutting of one's mouth to talk to the person one most loved. It was all such a tension.

139

She liked pears, anchovy paste, and honey. She tended to sit inelegantly, with acres of pink celonese knickers and red dimply flesh apparent. It was ages before she stopped having brown bread and butter or biscuits with her early morning tea. She had a vivid imagination. A graphic vocabulary. She ate up all the food on her plate, even if she was full, because of the refugees. She taught us to drive. She taught us to read, write, and tell the time before we went to school. I think she was innocent of orgasm, so maybe it's as well it will die out with me. She couldn't keep a secret, especially if she considered it unreasonable of one to want it kept. She believed it to be a kind of sacrilege for women to touch themselves between their legs. In the bath a flannel clothed the hand that washed. She argued extremely well. She was a keen Liberal. She liked change, and progress, and accepted it. She tackled difficulties. She didn't understand the ethic of being polite and gentle, within the family; she seemed to think one had a moral duty to express oneself, fiercely and freely, with zest and vigour. She crusaded, trampling cheerfully, and was surprised if people were hurt. The people concerned were daughters-in-law. She could be quite idiotic. She was energetic and brave. I hated her borrowing my books, because she twisted their spines reading them in bed.

I want to make sense of my life: don't let me alter my memory to suit my conscience. I nearly failed to stay the course. I tried to walk out, to extract myself, but at that opportune or shameful moment, she launched into the process of death.

I shut a toad into the threshold of the kitchen door, by mistake in the dark. It was there in the morning, neatly squashed in half.

140

I kept a puppy with joint evil alive, in a cardboard box, under a dull emitter, or in my bed, when I shouldn't have. In ignorance. It was a living bundle of pus.

Absent, the rats made their absence felt: in the dry, hollow runs, under the mud and brick floors of sheds; in the gnawing of the wood in the loft, the doors, the partitions; with old, desiccated droppings. It was easy to see the place had been infested with many families of rat; though they were gone.

A year later, they came to occupy. There was rather a lot of them; they came as a troop, and colonised us. I would heave a hay bale in the loft and put my hand on soft blobs. I heard rats scurrying to avoid me as I moved through the sheds and barn at night, feeding animals, or to lift a broody hen. It might be imagined we were dirty; we were not; foodstuff was in bins; no muck, no scraps, so they ate themselves a hole in the kitchen ceiling and stole the cats' dinners; they thumped and banged over our heads. The holes we blocked they unblocked. And gnawed others. Therefore reached the conservatory, where we might find an angelic-looking rat propped upright on the table, bold as can be. It was all alarmingly swift. The house was pervaded with a sense of nausea. The cats seemed helpless. The terrier killed odd members of the population. But the dogs were unable to see to the root of the matter, the rat citadel underground. The rats could be heard squeaking. The pest man had to be invited to minister poison, which he laid in the runs; he gave their deaths nasty touches; most rat death is unkind; rats are not kind: bloated bodies appeared, their dreadful agonies to be presumed. Beyond endurance, one is vicious. The rats were finished, rolled up. They left one of us with contagious hepatitis; and it was not me.

141

I simply felt guilty, without knowing why or what I should have done – sooner. I wasn't in horror of brown rats, I was accustomed to living around the occasional rat or two; rats the cats and dogs brought in and left dopey and reeling on the hearth rug; rats sneaking off into the darkness. It had been grotesque, out of control, out of due proportion. And it was harmful.

I dream of tortoises, babies with little shells and long black legs: they jump and hurtle themselves dangerously at my neck, clinging with their arms, their eyes shining, trying to express love.

Is one ever excluded from one's own dreams, excused from taking part? I might like that.

I dream of climbing to the top of a mountain in Switzerland and seeing Brazil. The hurt inside my eyes as they open to a dazzling light; not a terrestial landscape, a bronzed and glittering surface like armour; in scale, immense; though not such that the mind cannot grasp or the eye observe. I have intimate knowledge of it; a vision. And always the lens dilating to encompass the brilliant prospect. It bears no relation. I have been here before. But I have not.

I dream of mucus running from my cunt in a stream, flowing across the floor and out under the front door.

I have temptation dreams, with the strength to pull explicitly: I saw my neighbour, next to whom I have lived for five placid years, with a huge erection; come on, I said; and he did; we did; but while I was in his bed, a madwoman entered my flat, and devastated it. A notebook on my table, quite irreplaceable, was shrivelled to a wet, mouldy dust; like a warning from heaven; peril to disregard it.

I have four breasts, one full of lumps.

142

Or I wake with something I don't remember: exhausting and overwhelming anger and despair. Too much to contain: equally, too hopeless to expel from the body.

I dream of a fat man, with a belly smooth as an egg; I am consulting him in some fashion; he says I should come into hospital for nine days; and I say, I can't, I should go mad; and as he sits pondering, I put out my hand, and absent-mindedly stroke his unnatural protrusion; it is erotic, I find; and he begins to fuck me; and I think, he could be struck off, but he is trying to heal me.

I have beckoning dreams. They are the worst, and not welcome. I see my mother, or, more usually, my dog, standing some way from me on a little mound, a rise. There is silence. And this beckoning: the dog makes the gesture with his foreleg crooked, with his paw. I wake thinking, but they are *dead.*

If it is required of me to yield up the ghost, it ought to be as a punishment for morbidity.

Dreams of touching my breast and milk spurting from the nipple: milking it, filling tumblers with the milk of human un-kindness. I dream of orgasm.

Our dreams are not fodder for analysis; we take them to be a primary manifestation, in symbolic terms, of wish-fulfilment, dreads, and terrors: our minds are cleverer than ourselves; the dream is the achievement of a mind that has already dissected, it is the complete picture, in which the senses and the intellect are fused – in conscious day they are indifferently connected.

I dream of a garden, a large old red house. I am gardening but not the gardener, nor am I the owner. A dog with claws like a cat's, which it digs into me as I bend over, weeding. And twittering finches, of paradise colours, dying of poison by the hand of the jealous, the

143

real gardener. I look for a brick to knock them on the head with, in the nests they have formed in the long grass by their writhing. I have to remove the dog's claws from the seat of my trousers, and transport him to the door. I pass a tall window, which previously had seemed opaque; within are many books, mellow and leathery and with laminated jackets. I am hungry. I am *famished*. I wake before I have a chance to relieve the pain of the birds.

I shall tell myself a parable.

Once upon a time, there was a dog – to be precise, a bitch – who had to change her home at the age of three or four. She came to us on breeding terms. Outwardly, she made no fuss; but each day, she went down to the gate alone, and sat with her back to us, waiting. After she had sat and looked, she returned, expressionless. She was intelligent, and of great character. And when she at last knew that no one would fetch her away, she merely stopped her journeys to the gate, and lived cheerfully with us for the rest of her life.

There comes a time for making peace with oneself, and that peace is acceptance.

I should let things die: caring, and loving, and wanting. Life as I have known it is ending. I am drying up: the desire that has been pouring out of me all these years, wetting my knickers, is easing in its abundance. I am old, older, uglier, ugly. I have rings around my neck – hangman's wrinkles. I have wrists with shackle marks. I have pouches under the eyes to fit two baby kangaroos.

I shall step defiantly on to false teeth, grey hair, reading glasses, vaginal atrophy, and varicose veins. To the limbo before the pitiful energy that arrives with the knowledge of things left undone which never are to be done.

144

I fear the unimaginable loneliness of the spinster, but the actuality, I think, will be numbed by dear nature.

If I am troubled or sick, friends may be more troubled and sicker. I am not inclined to ask for magic.

Better to be aware one is alone. Better not to be deluded.

The wish to be dragged up the glen by a mammoth hairy bare-kneed Highlander, and fucked, must be firmly reconciled with the idea that I should not like it — the dragging, not the fucking. Fantasy is awkward stuff.

I do long to say 'we', not 'I'. But at least I can't remember ever wanting to be anyone other than myself; a deep, blood-red root of confidence. It has been no problem, identity; leant heavily upon, it was there; accessible. That's luck.

I don't have to define anything: I can put my hand out and touch. I am peeling off a transfer of myself. I am saying: here is a life, what do you make of it. And trying not to mind that you turn aside. I am, she would say, I should say, am saying, genuinely alive. An invisible bramble bush with six-inch thorns and poisonous berries, and prickles that cling like hell's sweetheart, tendrils . . . that may be what separates one plant from another, one tree, one copse . . . one wood.

In order to see one's own hands, as others see them, one has to twist them backwards on the wrist; and whereas before they were thin and elegant, they are now whiter, veinier, lumpier, and much older; the same with nails; the thumb nail looks straight; it's an illusion; it is not; it is sat crooked on its discontented flesh; and is misshapen.

No break, no warning, between calm contemplation, and mopping tears. I want to cry not in grief, in sadness, but with life, and sheer pleasure. I *shall* feel the substance of my skin change. It shall take on an opaque smoothness, swap its mottled gooseberry for a milky smile; my lips shall issue from within my mouth instead of dangling on my face; and in that I shall have not grooves of lead but little lines.

There are places in my dreams I have been acquainted with for years: sometimes trees have been felled, and fences erected.

On the 31st August, 1319, the outlaw Robin Hood climbed an oak at the edge of the forest; and sat out on a limb, eating an apple whose white flesh was stained with red as if from the streaks of its skin; the sky was blue; the leaves dark green, hiding shadows; fluffy clouds were buzzing along nicely in the breeze; it was a sharp day, with a tang of autumn: he wondered what gave autumn its smell; not dead leaves, for they still hung to the twigs, were not even yellow; not the cut corn, the sheaves, the threshing, because autumn smelt where no harvest was; not the animals, in summer coats; it must be, he thought, the fresh wind, the apples ripening, the flowers – a month to Michaelmas; there have been colder days; the sun is hot; but I can smell autumn. And towards the end of the fall, I shall smell winter, and in winter, spring; and in spring, summer.

Others, braver than I, hold their heads up.

I am stumbling into the future, wondering what to do with the rest of my life. That flame is a dangerous fallacy, a miasma, a putrefying gas from the marshes. But I have fuel enough in me to blaze alone.

Is Beauty Good
Rosalind Belben

Pre-publication acclaim for Rosalind Belben's new novel:

'*Is Beauty Good* is a wonderful book, subtle and intelligent. I can't think of anyone writing in English (with the possible exception of Beckett) whose prose is as beautiful. Each of the many voices resonates back and forth across the novel and charms with its wit and also its innocence. There is movement in the book, rather like the movement that seems to occur in medieval depictions of life cycles in which everything comes together and revolves.'   DAVID PLANTE.

'By not hurrying, by listening to each voice, almost speaking each word, a kind of world, absolutely solid yet always withheld from our gaze, makes itself felt. This book had an effect on me which was different from that of any other book I have ever read. It is a rare achievement, one to be treasured.'

GABRIEL JOSIPOVICI

'It is a beautiful work ... it says a great deal about the world we live in ... more life-like and more alive than most fiction.'   MICHAEL HAMBURGER

128 pages £6.95 (paper)

Also published by Serpent's Tail

The Seven Deadly Sins
Alison Fell (ed.)

'Seven fine writers, seven vices probed to the quick.
Splendid.'   ANGELA CARTER

'These seven writers represent . . . a newer and more
knowing feminist strategy . . . Mischievous and
exhilarating.'   LORNA SAGE, *The Observer*

'Rich in experiment and imagination, a sign of just
how far contemporary women's writing might go.'
                              HELEN BIRCH, *City Limits*

'All of these stories cut deeply and with a sharp edge
into the main business of life — death, God and the
devil.'   RICHARD NORTH, *New Musical Express*

'A rich but random survey of recent women's
writing.'   JONATHAN COE, *The Guardian*

'An exciting, imaginative mix of stories.'
                              ELIZABETH BURNS, *The List*

'Witty, modern, female.'
                       KATHLEEN JAMIE, *Scotland on Sunday*

'Extremely entertaining.'
                              EMMA DALLY, *Cosmopolitan*
                       240 pages £7.00 (paper)